memory's gate

Other books in the Time Thriller Trilogy

Ripple Effect (Book One)

Out of Time (Book Two)

time thriller trilogy

memory's gate

paul mccusker

ZONDERVAN®

ZONDERVAN.com/
AUTHORTRACKER
follow your favorite authors

We want to hear from you. Please send your comments about this book to us in care of zreview@zondervan.com. Thank you.

ZONDERVAN

Memory's Gate
Copyright © 2009 by Paul McCusker

Requests for information should be addressed to:
Zondervan, *Grand Rapids, Michigan* 49530

Library of Congress Cataloging-in-Publication Data

McCusker, Paul, 1958 –
    Memory's gate / Paul McCusker.
        p. cm. — (Time thriller trilogy ; bk. 3)
        Summary: Fifteen-year-old Elizabeth volunteers in a retirement home where a con man promises the elderly that they can slip through a time fault line and return to their past.
        ISBN 978-0-310-71438-5 (softcover)
        [1. Old age — Fiction. 2. Time travel — Fiction. 3. Christian life — Fiction.] I. Title.
PZ7.M47841635Me 2009
[Fic] — dc22   2009000826

Published in association with the literary agency of Alive Communications, Inc., 7680 Goddard Street, Suite 200, Colorado Springs, CO 80920. www.alivecommunications.com

Interior design by Christine Orejuela-Winkelman

Printed in the United States of America

---

09 10 11 12 13 14 15 • 23 22 21 20 19 18 17 16 15 14 13 12 11 10 9 8 7 6 5 4 3 2 1

To Rob and Di Parsons, for introducing me to St. Fagans and starting this adventure.

Prologue

George sat in the guest chair across from the massive oak desk, cradling a cup of hot coffee in his hands. His fingernails were dirty, he noticed, and the knees on his overalls were threadbare. These facts came as no surprise. Mopping and scrubbing the hospital for nine, sometimes ten hours a day was bound to get your fingernails filthy and wear your clothes out.

"What can I do for you, George?" Dr. Forbes, the hospital's staff psychologist, asked pleasantly.

George looked up and peered directly into Dr. Forbes' eyes. "It's all come back to me again," he said softly.

"Your fantasies?" Dr. Forbes asked.

George paused, biting his tongue to keep from responding to the word *fantasies*. They weren't fantasies. They were his memories. Instead of reacting, he simply nodded. "I think something is going to happen."

"Like what?"

"I'm going back to my ... to that other world."

Dr. Forbes raised an eyebrow. "Oh?"

"Everything is flooding back. Almost as if my life is flashing before my eyes."

"Your life in that other time," Dr. Forbes said.

"Yes."

"A life you claim to have lived over thirty years ago, George."

"I know. But it's as real to me as if it happened thirty minutes ago."

"What seems real? What, specifically, are you thinking about?"

"Everything. My family's tobacco farm — the acres and acres of land. My father's disappointment when I didn't want to go into the family business. My experiences in the Vietnam War."

"Which war?"

George smiled. In this world, in this time, the Vietnam War hadn't happened. But he had fought in it in his time, and when he'd returned from those jungles, he had built a house on twenty acres and married Julia, his childhood sweetheart. They even had two children: Susan and Donald.

"George?" Dr. Forbes coaxed him. "Is it wise to indulge yourself so much?"

"Probably not. But I think something is going to happen."

"You've been saying that for as long as I've known you."

"This time it's different."

"You said that a few months ago when they brought that girl in. What was her name? The amnesiac."

"They called her Sarah. But her real name was Elizabeth. She was from my time."

"So you said." Dr. Forbes spoke in a very measured and calming tone. "Though the girl denies ever calling herself Elizabeth. She says her name is Sarah."

"That's because her name *is* Sarah. She was a time twin. Elizabeth slipped back to her — my — time. And Sarah came back here."

"I see."

"I feel it now, just like I did when Elizabeth was here. Something is going to happen."

Dr. Forbes smiled. "It gives you hope, doesn't it?"

"What does?"

"The belief that one day you'll go back to this so-called *other time*."

George now knew it had been a mistake to confess all this to Dr. Forbes. Now they would be watching him closely again. They might even admit him for treatment. He didn't want that.

"How are you physically?" Dr. Forbes asked.

"You mean my heart?"

"Yes. Isn't that when this first started? That first heart attack?"

George nodded. The morning he had disappeared from his time, he had just said good-bye to his wife and children and was walking from the front porch to the gate. Dr. Beckett, the local vet, had driven up in his old Buick to look over one of the horses that wasn't eating properly. There was a young boy in the car — an English kid who visited in the summers to help out. George had turned to walk toward the car and within seconds he'd felt a numbness in his chest and knew that he'd inherited his father's bad heart. That's when he wound up here — in this other time.

He woke up in the hospital. The victim of a heart attack, they said. Probably from all the stress he endured daily as a stockbroker.

A stockbroker? But he was a farmer, he told them. He didn't know the first thing about stock — unless it was the kind of stock you fed and watered.

It's the trauma, they said. Heart attacks cause that. It's a form of amnesia.

No, he told them. I really am a farmer. Just ask my wife.

What wife? You're not married, they said.

And for the next few years they told him again and again that the life he remembered was all in his imagination — a bizarre side effect from the heart attack. He fought them at first, only to be told he was insane. Eventually he agreed to everything, just to get his freedom back, and took on the life they claimed was his.

But privately, he continued to hope. When Elizabeth came along, he knew the truth — what he had believed was real. There *was* another time, another world. Better still, it was possible to go back there. She'd done it — why couldn't he? One day he would. He just knew it.

Dr. Forbes was staring at him. "George?"

George looked back at him, putting on a contrite expression. "I'm sorry, Dr. Forbes. I'm being ridiculous. It's the long hours I put in here. I get stressed and I fantasize about going to that other time. That's all this is."

"It's your happy place," the doctor said. "We all need one. Mine is on a beach with white sand, blue seas, and clear skies."

George chuckled. "Thank you for listening, Doctor. It helps to be able to talk to someone. Anyone else would think I'm crazy."

"Take a vacation, George. I'm sure you're due one. I'll talk to the hospital chief about it."

"Thanks."

The meeting was over, and George made his way out of the doctor's office. He was crazy, all right. Crazy George. That's what Elizabeth had called him.

He was crazy to have hope. But he did.

Something was about to happen.

1

What in the world am I doing here? Elizabeth Forde asked herself as she followed a silver-haired woman down the cold, clinical main hallway of the Fawlt Line Retirement Center.

Of all the things I could have spent the rest of my summer doing, why this? Yes, she had agreed to volunteer at the retirement center. She had even felt enthusiastic about the idea at the time. But walking down the pale green hallway that smelled of pine disinfectant and aging bodies, Elizabeth wondered if she had made a mistake.

She'd been swept along by Reverend Armstrong's passionate call to the young people of the church. He had exuberantly insisted that they get involved in the community. They must be a generation of givers rather than takers, he'd said. His words were powerful and persuasive, and before she knew what she was doing she had joined a line of other young people to sign up for volunteer service. Just a few hours a day, three or four days a week, for a couple of weeks. It hadn't sounded like much.

An old man, bent over like a question mark, stepped out of his room and smiled toothlessly at her.

It's too much, she thought. *Let me out of here.*

"I know what you're thinking," said her guide, Mrs. Kottler, with a smile. "You're thinking that a few hours a day simply won't be enough. You'll want more time. Everyone feels that way. But if you do the best you can with the hours you have, you'll be just fine. I promise. Maybe later, once you've proven yourself, we'll let you come in longer."

Elizabeth smiled noncommittally.

Mrs. Kottler wore masterfully applied makeup, discreet gold jewelry, and a fashionable dark blue dress. She smelled of expensive perfume. Elizabeth thought she looked more like a real estate agent than the administrator of an old folks' home.

"We don't call it an 'old folks home,' by the way," Mrs. Kottler said, as if she'd read Elizabeth's mind, "or a 'sanitarium' or any of those other outdated names. It's just what the sign says: it's a retirement center. People have productive and active lives here. Being a senior citizen doesn't mean you have one foot in the grave. People who retire at sixty-five often have another twenty or thirty years to enjoy. We're here to help them live those years as fully as they can."

Elizabeth glanced at a couple of *productive* and *active* residents staring blankly at the television sets in their rooms.

"Of course, we do have *older* residents who have gone beyond their mental or physical capacity to jog around the center six times a day, if you know what I mean," Mrs. Kottler added as they rounded a corner and walked briskly down a short corridor toward two large doors. "For everyone else, there's a full schedule of activities throughout the day. Most take place here in the recreation room."

Mrs. Kottler pushed on the two doors, which swung open grandly to reveal a large room filled with game tables, easels, a large-screen television, and bookcases filled with hundreds of books and magazines. Unlike the main halls and cafeteria Elizabeth had just seen, this room was decorated warmly with wooden end tables, lace doilies, and the kinds of chairs and sofas found in showcase living rooms. Tastefully painted scenes of sunlit hills, lush green valleys, and golden rivers adorned the walls.

"Pretty, huh? I decorated this one myself," Mrs. Kottler said. "I know what you're thinking. You're thinking that they should have let me decorate the entire center. Well, that wasn't my decision to make. The residents are responsible for decorating their own rooms any way they like. Most of the other assembly areas were done before I joined the staff."

"How long have you been working here?" Elizabeth asked politely.

"Five years," Mrs. Kottler answered. She added wistfully, "Time. It goes by so quickly, don't you find?"

For Elizabeth, who had been only eleven when Mrs. Kottler started her job, the last five years hadn't gone by quickly at all. She had traveled from the carefree days of Barbie dolls to the insecurities of middle school and now to young adulthood and wide-eyed wonder over her future. And she had also traveled to a parallel time — not that she'd be inclined to mention such a thing to Mrs. Kottler. *No, it hasn't gone by very quickly*, she thought. And as she considered the residents of the center and realized that one day *she* might have to live in a place like this, she hoped life would never go by that quickly. She shuddered at the thought.

As Elizabeth was contemplating, a tall, handsome young man entered through a door at the opposite end of the recreation room. "Mrs. K, I was wondering — "

"Doug Hall, come meet Elizabeth Forde," Mrs. Kottler said, waving her arms as if she might create enough of a breeze to sail Doug over to them.

Doug strode across the room with a smile that showed off the deep dimples in his cheeks. *He's got to be a movie star*, Elizabeth thought. His curly brown hair, perfectly formed face, large brown eyes, and painstakingly sculpted physique was only enhanced by the white clinical coat. *He's a movie star playing a doctor*, she decided.

Doug stretched out his hand and said, "Well, my enjoyment of this place just increased by a hundred percent."

She shook his hand and blushed. "Hi."

"Doug is our maintenance engineer," Mrs. Kottler explained.

Doug smiled again. "She means I'm the main janitor. But I'm more like a bouncer, in case these old merrymakers get out of control with their wild partying and carousing."

"Stop it, Doug," Mrs. Kottler said with a giggle, then turned to Elizabeth. "I know what you're thinking. You're wondering what a good-looking, charming young man like him is doing in a place like this. Right?"

For once, Mrs. Kottler had it right. *He's a movie star playing a janitor?* It didn't seem appropriate somehow. She waited for the answer.

"Well, if you find out, please let me know," Mrs. Kottler said with another giggle. "He won't tell anyone. I assume he has a deep, dark secret. Perhaps he was involved in some sort of intrigue in France and barely escaped from the police on his yacht. Why else would he be doing maintenance in a retirement center in a small town?"

"If you must know the truth, I ran off with the church funds," Doug said. He and Mrs. Kottler chuckled as if this little exchange had been their own private joke for a long time.

Doug rested his gaze on Elizabeth, making her feel self-conscious. How did she look in her freshly issued pink-and-white clinic jacket — frumpy or professional? Had she taken enough time with her makeup? Were her large brown eyes properly accented? Did her smile look natural? Her skin was freshly tanned, and she had no zits today, thank goodness. She'd tied back her long brown hair, but now she wished she had let it fall loose. It looked better that way, Jeff always said.

Jeff.

Thinking of her boyfriend right then made her pause — as if

her self-conscious vanity was, in and of itself, disloyal to him. She glanced away from Doug quickly.

"Well, back to business," Doug said pleasantly, as if he'd picked up on her feelings and wanted to spare her any embarrassment. "I was wondering if now would be a good time to adjust the settings on the Jacuzzi. You don't have any plans to let the big kids in this afternoon, right?"

"No, Doug, the *kids* won't be going in today," Mrs. Kottler replied, smiling. "Do whatever you need to do."

He nodded. "Maybe Elizabeth will want to test it later when I'm finished." He raised his eyebrows and flashed a mischievous grin.

"I think Elizabeth will be too busy getting acclimated to her new duties," Mrs. Kottler replied.

Doug tipped a finger against his brow as a farewell. "If there's anything I can do to help ..."

Mrs. Kottler watched him go. "He's such a flirt. A charming, good-looking flirt, but a flirt nonetheless." Elizabeth detected a hint of jealousy in her voice.

The tour of the center eventually led Elizabeth and Mrs. Kottler outside to the five acres of manicured grounds, landscaped into gentle green slopes that ultimately rolled down to Richards Lake. The small, manmade lake was enclosed on one side by a natural forest that extended off to the horizon. Elizabeth walked alongside Mrs. Kottler, feeling oppressed by the humidity of the August afternoon. She swatted at the occasional mosquito that tried to make a meal of her arms.

"The heat and mosquitoes tend to keep everyone inside on days like this," Mrs. Kottler said.

"Except those two," Elizabeth said, gesturing to two people in a white Victorian-style gazebo near the lake.

"That's Sheriff Hounslow and his father," Mrs. Kottler said with just enough annoyance to betray her usual professional detachment. "I suppose we should say a quick hello."

As they got closer, Elizabeth saw that the sheriff, a large man in a light gray uniform, was pacing agitatedly. His father, a shadow from this distance, was sitting on one of the benches that lined the gazebo. Sheriff Hounslow saw them coming and waved.

Mrs. Kottler spoke to Elizabeth in a low voice. "The sheriff's father, Adam Hounslow, joined us just a couple of days ago. Like many new residents, he's having a hard time adjusting. Hello, Sheriff!"

Mrs. Kottler and Elizabeth mounted the steps to the shade underneath the round white roof covering the gazebo.

"Look who's here," Sheriff Hounslow announced. "Mrs. Kottler and — well, well — Elizabeth Forde."

"Oh, you know my new volunteer? Elizabeth will be with us a few hours a day for the next couple of weeks."

"That's nice. You be sure to take special care of my father," the sheriff said, nodding toward the older man. Elizabeth could see the old man clearly now. His frame was stooped with age and arthritis, and he had a pale, wrinkled face with hazel eyes. Wisps of thin white hair sprayed out from a spotted crown, and he scowled at them, deep frown lines etching his forehead. Elizabeth could clearly see the resemblance between father and son — in their features and their demeanor.

"Wouldn't you like a pretty girl like Elizabeth to help take care of you, Dad?" the sheriff asked.

"I don't need to be taken care of," the old man growled. He tucked his head down against his chest.

Sheriff Hounslow ignored the remark and continued. "I'm surprised to see you here, Elizabeth. Shouldn't you be getting ready for the grand opening of that historical amusement park, or whatever Malcolm calls it?"

"It's not an amusement park," Elizabeth corrected him. "It's called the Historical Village."

"I didn't know you were connected to Malcolm Dubbs." Mrs. Kottler said, impressed. Malcolm Dubbs was the closest thing

Fawlt Line had to royalty, a member of the family that had been in the area for nearly 300 years. Malcolm came from England to manage the Dubbs estate after the last American adult member of the Dubbs family had been killed.

"She's also dating Malcolm's cousin, Jeff Dubbs," the sheriff informed her.

"Are you? Doug will be very disappointed," Mrs. Kottler teased, then said earnestly, "Jeff's parents died in that terrible plane crash, didn't they? That was so sad. I think Malcolm Dubbs is a remarkable man. Imagine taking in that boy."

"*That boy* is the true heir to the entire Dubbs estate," the sheriff interjected. "If I were him, I'd have a lot of trouble with cousin Malcolm using *my* money to build that park."

"It's not Jeff's money unless Malcolm dies," Elizabeth corrected him. "He's entitled to do whatever he wants with it. And Jeff is very proud of Malcolm."

Mrs. Kottler nodded. "After all, Malcolm is using it to create something educational for everyone. It's not as if he's squandering it." She turned to Elizabeth. "Is it true that he's brought in buildings, displays, and artifacts from all over the world?"

"Whatever he can find. As much as he could find from the past few hundred years, from picture frames and hairbrushes to schoolhouses and church ruins." Elizabeth covered a smile, realizing she had just recited from one of Malcolm's brochures. "Phase One opens on Saturday."

"Phase One?"

"Malcolm says the village is a work in progress. He'll open various sections of it as they're ready."

"Like I said, it's an amusement park of history," the sheriff said dismissively.

Elizabeth frowned at Sheriff Hounslow, knowing better than most the adversarial relationship he had with Malcolm. Elizabeth suspected that the sheriff was jealous of Malcolm's wealth and the respect he commanded from the townspeople. Whatever the reason, Hounslow never missed an opportunity to poke fun at Malcolm's projects and eccentricities.

"I can't wait to go on the rides!" he added.

"Are there rides?" Mrs. Kottler asked, confused.

Elizabeth shook her head. "No. Just buildings and displays."

Sheriff Hounslow continued. "There's going to be a big celebration. The mayor will be there as well as a special assistant to the governor, and there'll be a telegram from the president and maybe even world peace — all thanks to Malcolm Dubbs. Ha!"

"Don't be such a pompous fool, Richard," Adam Hounslow barked at his son. "I'm looking forward to seeing the village."

"I'm glad you're looking forward to something," the sheriff muttered.

"Now that you've stuck me in a place like this, I'm lucky to look forward to anything," Adam snapped in return.

"Oh, I'm sure you don't mean that," Mrs. Kottler said. "The Fawlt Line Retirement Center will be like home to you in no time at all, I promise."

Adam scowled. "This will never be my home. My home has been sold right out from under me by my thoughtful and compassionate son."

"I'm not getting into this argument with you again, Dad," Hounslow said irritably.

"Yes you are," Adam replied. "As long as you are forcing me to live in a place I don't want to live, we'll have this argument."

The sheriff turned on his father. "Where else are you going to live? You couldn't stay in that big old place alone. You can barely take care of yourself, let alone keep up with a big house."

The old man snorted and turned away.

Sheriff Hounslow kept at it. "Do I have to remind you what led up to this? Do I have to announce to the whole world how you nearly burned the house down — twice — by forgetting to turn the stove burners off? Or the time you flooded the house by wandering off to the store while the bath water was running?"

Mrs. Kottler caught Elizabeth's eyes and jerked her head toward the center, signaling that they should leave. Heading across the grounds, Elizabeth could still hear the voices of the two men arguing behind her.

"I know what you're thinking," Mrs. Kottler said. "You're thinking that Adam must be crazy not to like our center. Well, I agree. Not to worry, though. He'll get used to it. They always do."

They approached the building from the back, where a stone patio filled with flowering plants had been added to the recreation room. A man in a wheelchair was pruning the plants, meticulously spraying the leaves with a water bottle and wiping them. He had long gray hair that poured out from under a large baseball cap. Beneath the brim, he wore sunglasses so dark that Elizabeth couldn't see his eyes at all. A bushy mustache and beard flowed downward. It struck her that, apart from his cheeks, his face was entirely covered. He wore a baggy jogging suit that, to Elizabeth's thinking, must have been terribly hot.

"That's Mr. Betterman, another new resident," Mrs. Kottler said. "Come meet him."

They crossed the patio and Mrs. Kottler introduced them.

Mr. Betterman didn't speak, but grunted and held a carnation out to her.

"Very nice," Elizabeth said.

"Take it," Mrs. Kottler whispered.

Elizabeth reached out to take the flower. For a second he didn't let go, but used the moment to lean closer to her and whisper, "I know who you are." He gave her a slight smile, then turned away to fiddle with the planter.

Disconcerted, Elizabeth looked to Mrs. Kottler, who gently shrugged as they walked inside.

"I wonder what he meant by that?" Mrs. Kottler mused, once they were inside and out of Mr. Betterman's hearing.

"I don't know," Elizabeth replied, but something about the man's half-smile and voice seemed familiar to her somehow.

"Still, it was an honor that he singled you out, you know," Mrs. Kottler said. "He doesn't usually talk to anyone. He's a little eccentric."

No kidding, Elizabeth thought.

As they drifted through the recreation room, Elizabeth found herself looking for the handsome maintenance man. She wasn't a flirt — nor was she interested in anyone but Jeff — yet she was drawn to Doug. She wasn't sure why ... Elizabeth shook her head to clear it and turned her attention back to Mrs. Kottler, who was finishing the tour..

Mrs. Kottler smiled proudly. "Well, that's most of it. I know what you're thinking. You're thinking this is more like a beautiful hotel than a retirement center, right? Well, we do our best. Now let me show you where the storage closets are and introduce you to your new responsibilities."

2

Malcolm Dubbs lived in a cottage on the edge of the family's vast estate, bordering the north edge of the town of Fawlt Line. It had a manor house built in the 17th century, which was now part of the Historical Village. The cottage reminded him of England, and it fit him and Jeff perfectly. Elizabeth thought the two were remarkably happy, considering the tragedy that had brought them together.

Tall and slender, Malcolm was sitting at the large desk in his den when Elizabeth and Jeff arrived. The sun was soon to set, and a dim yellow light washed over the cluttered room. Thanks to the oak tree just beyond the French doors leading out to the patio, drops of cooler, green light filtered into the room. The rays highlighted the old-fashioned furniture and skimmed along the dark wood paneling, the classic paintings, the shelves sagging under too many books. Jeff smiled and turned on the banker's lamp at the head of the desk.

Malcolm looked up and blinked at Jeff. "Oh, hi," he said with a start. "Good evening, Elizabeth." His British accent made him sound intelligent and genteel.

"Good evening, Malcolm," Elizabeth said.

"Are you all right?" Jeff asked, noticing the small worry lines on his cousin's face.

Malcolm sighed. "All the preparations for the grand opening have left me with too much to do and too little time."

Jeff gestured to the papers on the desk. "What are you working on now?"

Malcolm pushed the papers away wearily. "These are daily reports of completed projects within the Village, and this is another report discussing the security system and inherent weaknesses. It appears that some areas remain vulnerable to theft."

"Vulnerable?" Elizabeth asked.

"The security cameras still aren't working." Malcolm leaned back in his chair and shoved his hands into the pockets of his tweed sports coat. He stretched his long legs as far as they would go.

"It's not all doom and gloom, I hope," Elizabeth said.

"No. The eighteenth-century windmill from Holland is working perfectly. And we wrapped up the construction on the miners' row houses from southwest Pennsylvania. I'm particularly proud of that exhibit."

"Why that one?"

Malcolm smiled. "Because it shows the chronology of change better than most of the displays. You start at one end of the row houses, and as you walk through each one you'll see exactly how the miners lived during the last 180 years. Go in the first door, and you'll see how it was in 1820. Move to the next door and you're looking at 1840, then 1860, 1880 and so on until you come to the present day. We spent a lot of time getting every detail just right."

Elizabeth shook her head. "I don't know how you pulled it all together."

"Sometimes I wonder myself," Malcolm admitted. "It's been a long time in the making."

"Hundreds of years, I figure," Jeff said.

Malcolm waved his hand to change the subject. "Forget

about the Village for now. How was your first day as a volunteer, Elizabeth?"

Elizabeth was pleased that he remembered, considering all the other demands on his mind, but that was typical Malcolm. "It was mostly just a chance to look around. I only met a couple of people. The center is nice, I guess, if you have to live in a place like that."

Malcolm chuckled. "Your faint praise is underwhelming."

Jeff dropped onto the sofa across from the desk and ran his hands through his wavy dark hair. "She's sorry she ever volunteered."

"Jeff . . ." Elizabeth sent him a sharp look.

"What?" Jeff asked innocently. "Did I say something wrong?"

Malcolm stood up and smiled sympathetically. "If it's any consolation, Elizabeth, I think volunteering to help out at a retirement center is a noble and difficult thing to do. Many retirement homes are downright depressing, and elderly people can be very unpredictable, depending on their states of mind. But if you remember that they're people, and not just old people, you have the opportunity to do them a world of good."

Elizabeth thought of how Doug Hall called the residents "kids" and probably charmed the socks off them, if only because he didn't treat them differently from anyone else.

"As quirky as your parents are, you should feel right at home," Jeff said with a laugh. Elizabeth kicked at his ankle before sitting next to him on the sofa.

Malcolm tugged at his ear thoughtfully. "I haven't been out to the center since they renovated it. When I was a kid, it wasn't a retirement home. It was just a house on a farm. In fact, it was owned by someone you two have heard a lot about."

Elizabeth and Jeff looked at each other blankly.

"That's where the Richards property is," Malcolm said. "It's where Charles Richards disappeared."

The two teens' faces lit up with the realization.

"You mean *the* Charles Richards?" Jeff asked.

"The one who disappeared like I did?" Elizabeth added.

Malcolm nodded. The three of them looked at each other silently as the story and the memories came flooding back.

✿ ✿ ✿

The legend of Charles Richards had been whispered about around Fawlt Line for thirty years, and the mystery surrounding his sudden disappearance had never been solved. At this point, most people considered it just a small-town myth — like haunted houses and the bogeyman. But Malcolm, Elizabeth, and Jeff knew that Charles Richards was more than a myth. They knew what had happened to him was very real, because Malcolm had witnessed the disappearance firsthand.

When Malcolm was a boy, he visited his American relatives in Fawlt Line every summer. Early one morning, he was helping the local veterinarian Hezekiah Beckett run errands. They drove up to the front of the Richards' home, just as Charles Richards stepped out of the front door and kissed his wife Julia good-bye. He patted his two children's heads as he passed them and made his way down the sidewalk toward the front gate. Then, without sound or any change in his surroundings, he suddenly disappeared.

Horrified, Julia, the kids, Dr. Beckett and Malcolm raced to the spot where Charles had just been standing, but saw only the fence and the grass. There were no bushes or trees for him to hide behind, no holes to fall into, nothing to explain how he could simply vanish. Yet no trace of him could be found anywhere.

Julia was bedridden for months afterward, lost in the hope that her husband would return. No funeral or memorial service was ever held, but Charles never came back. Later, the family sold the farm and moved away.

The event changed Malcolm's life, giving him a passion for

history, quantum physics, theories of time travel, and unexplained phenomenon. The theory he had settled on after studying other strange stories in Fawlt Line's history was that the town was actually a *fault line* into other times or dimensions. He was convinced that Charles Richards had fallen through that fault. He had never been seen again — or had he?

✿ ✿ ✿

Elizabeth felt a chill go up and down her spine as thoughts of Charles Richards reminded her of her own experience, when *she* became a victim of the time fault. She stood up and walked to the window, her arms folded tightly around her.

"Bits?" Jeff asked, worried.

"I'm all right," she said softly. The day was fading, the shadows stretching, as Elizabeth remembered that strange night.

While taking a bath a year ago, she had slipped through a fracture in time and wound up in a parallel Fawlt Line where everyone thought she was a girl named Sarah. She insisted that she was really Elizabeth and ended up in a hospital being treated as an amnesiac. Because so many people thought she was Sarah, Elizabeth had almost given in to believing she *was* Sarah, even though her memories told her otherwise.

But then on Elizabeth's side of the fault line, a girl was found unconscious who looked exactly like Elizabeth but clearly *wasn't* Elizabeth — different dental records, for one thing — which led Malcolm to work out a theory that Elizabeth and Sarah were sort of "time twins" who had switched places.

Elizabeth shivered and rubbed her arms absently. That she had made it back to Fawlt Line — her Fawlt Line — was nothing short of a miracle. She nearly lost her life. But Jeff and Malcolm had put Malcolm's theory to the test and saved her. Well, they'd had some help from a man at the hospital on the other side of the fault.

✿ ✿ ✿

Elizabeth sighed deeply from her place at the window. She hardly noticed that Jeff was now at her side.

"What are you thinking about?" he asked.

"Crazy George," she said.

While she was stuck in that other time, Elizabeth had met a maintenance worker at the hospital who insisted that he had also made the switch from one time to the other. At first she didn't believe him and had called him Crazy George. But he ultimately saved her life from an attempted murder. It was a nightmarish experience, and only in the end did she realize Crazy George wasn't crazy at all.

"He's still trapped there," she said now to Jeff. "Just like Charles Richards and only God knows how many others — Sweet, old Crazy George is trapped in that other time."

Elizabeth felt the tears form in her eyes. She hardly talked about her time travel experience because of the sadness and anxiety it brought her. Even now, as she sat in the security of Malcolm's study, it upset her. In the deepest part of her heart, she feared that the nightmare might return just by bringing it up too much. Because even though Malcolm had figured out *what* was happening, he hadn't figured out what *made* it happen — or if and when it would happen again.

Jeff hugged her close, then turned his attention back to Malcolm. "What happened to the Richards' house since then?"

"They tore it down and built a gaudy mansion on the site. It was the kind of place kids liked to throw rocks at. Then they tore *that* down and put up the new building a couple of years ago. How does it look inside?"

Elizabeth didn't answer, her mind still on Crazy George and her own frightening adventure.

"Bits?" Jeff asked, rubbing her arm gently.

Elizabeth shook her head, focusing on Malcolm's question. "It's ... modern. Just one story with a lot of hallways. More like a hospital than a home."

Jeff and Malcolm glanced warily at each other.

"What's wrong?" she asked.

"I think you should go home," Malcolm suggested. "You must be tired from your first day."

"No, really — I'm all right," she said.

But Jeff held out his hand. "Come on, Bits. Really, you should get home."

Elizabeth looked at him curiously, then took his hand and followed him to the door.

✿ ✿ ✿

Jeff brought his Volkswagen to a squeaky stop in front of Elizabeth's house and turned off the headlights. They looked up at the front window and saw Alan Forde pacing in the living room, waving his hands and talking animatedly.

"Is he lecturing someone?" Jeff asked.

Elizabeth shook her head. "Sort of. He's been recording a series of talks about the legends of King Arthur."

"Recording them for whom?"

"Anyone who wants them," she answered. "He's been obsessed with Arthur ever since ... well, you know."

The "you know" was a reference to yet another Fawlt Line adventure — when the legendary King Arthur had slipped through the fault line and ended up in — well, Fawlt Line. Malcolm and Jeff ended up escorting the king back to England, where he and his sword Excalibur slipped back through time.

"I'd like to hear what your dad has to say about the good King Arthur, especially since I got to know him myself," Jeff said.

Elizabeth glanced at Jeff gratefully. "He'd be happy if you asked."

"I'll wait for some other time. Right now, I want you to tell me what's going on with you."

Elizabeth hadn't expected such a direct question, though she should have. Jeff could always tell when something was wrong.

Sometimes it was a comfort to her that her longtime friend, who was now her boyfriend, knew her so well. Other times it made her feel uneasy, particularly when she didn't have an answer — like tonight. "I don't know," she said after a long pause.

"You must have a clue," he probed.

She turned in the seat to face him. "I really don't know, Jeff. Maybe it's just volunteering at the center. It was so ... strange. At first I thought it was because I don't know anything about helping old people. But then ..."

"But then what?"

She struggled over what to say next. "Sheriff Hounslow's father is a resident there, and the two of them were arguing and it was embarrassing ... and then I met a guy in a wheelchair who gave me a carnation, and he said he knew me."

Jeff grimaced. "He knows you? How?"

"He didn't say, and I was too surprised to ask. It was really weird. I had this feeling that I'd seen him before, but I don't know where."

Jeff took her hand in his and spoke softly. "Look, Malcolm's probably right. Old folks can be unpredictable, and that makes you nervous. Do you remember how Grandpa Dubbs was before he died?"

Elizabeth nodded. "He kept accusing the servants of stealing things."

"Because he kept forgetting where he put them," Jeff finished. "It used to scare the wits out of me when he launched into one of his tirades. Maybe the guy in the wheelchair really thought he knew you, but he was thinking of someone else. Probably someone from his past."

Elizabeth agreed silently.

"I'm just guessing, but it gave you the creeps to find out that the retirement center was built on Charles Richards' place, right?"

"It brought back a lot more than I wanted to remember."

"That's what I figured." Jeff was quiet for a moment. His expression told Elizabeth that he was forming his words carefully before speaking. "Maybe ... you should get some counseling about ... what happened to you — and me. Maybe we all should."

"Oh, right," Elizabeth said, unamused. "I can see me now in the first session with the counselor: 'Well, I'm here because I traveled to a parallel time ... and my time twin went to my time. I almost got killed, but my boyfriend also traveled in time, and his time twin showed up in Fawlt Line too.' Yeah, that'll work. He'll have me committed just like the doctor there, uh, *then* wanted to do."

"I'm just saying that getting bounced around in time and going through what you went through can't be healthy."

"You're right about that."

"I mean, especially since you don't like to talk about it."

"I'm okay, Jeff," Elizabeth insisted. "I think it's just today, volunteering at the center, bumping into some weird people, and then thinking about Charles Richards and Crazy George. Maybe I am just tired. I'll be all right, really ..."

✿ ✿ ✿

But Elizabeth knew she wasn't all right. She had a hard time falling asleep that night, as images of Crazy George spun through her mind and mixed with scenes from the Fawlt Line Retirement Center. Mrs. Kottler kept saying, "I know what you're thinking," and then Doug Hall offered her flowers that had been carefully pruned by the wheelchair-bound Mr. Betterman. The floor of the retirement home then opened up to expose a dark, cavernous time fault that threatened to pull her in. She fell — and never stopped falling.

Elizabeth sat up suddenly in bed, gasping and shaking. She knew that one way or another, she had to take back her offer to volunteer at the center.

3

Elizabeth spent most of the next day trying to figure out how to get out of helping at the retirement center gracefully. She knew her parents expected her to be responsible and not quit without a good reason. The challenge was to find a good and plausible reason. School hadn't started yet, so she couldn't blame homework. She had no other jobs or commitments, so she couldn't say her schedule was too busy. One by one she came up with excuses. One by one her better judgment knocked them down.

Even up to the moment when her mother dropped her off at the center, Elizabeth was trying to come up with a story that would justify telling Mrs. Kottler that she couldn't be there. But nothing came to mind. Despondently, she kissed her mother on the cheek and climbed out of the car. Her only hope — and fear — was that something might happen during her shift that would provide a solid way out.

Once inside, Mrs. Kottler gave her a simple assignment to take the serving cart around and fill the water jugs in all the rooms.

Elizabeth guessed that this was a standard job for new volunteers and a shrewd way to help them get to know the residents. Many were up and about when Elizabeth walked into the various rooms and community areas. It was her first full view of the people she would be assisting. While some were kind and welcoming, others regarded her with wariness or skepticism. *Just like kids on the first day of school*, she thought. *You can't tell about people until you get to know them better.* That was a good way to think about them, she decided. They were just older kids watching a new student.

But these "students" sure looked different from the ones at her school. Elizabeth was instantly struck by the tufts of white hair and varying styles of hairpieces worn by both the men and women. Her next impression was that many were quite agile, moving quickly and freely up and down the hallway, in and out of chairs, without the stiff or stooped gait she expected from older people. Some used canes and walkers, while others simply steadied themselves against whatever sturdy objects happened to be nearby. *They're just people*, Elizabeth reminded herself as they chatted amiably among themselves, played games in the recreation room or strolled thoughtfully alone. There were others, of course, who were less capable and needed more attention and care. Sharp minds were encased in fragile bodies. Sharp bodies sometimes encased fragile minds. It varied from room to room, person to person.

The most uncomfortable moment came when she reached Adam Hounslow's room. The door was slightly ajar, and she could see through the crack that the room was dark. The blinds had been drawn, and Adam was talking to someone in a wheelchair. Though his back was to her, Elizabeth recognized the baseball cap and knew it was Mr. Betterman. The men spoke in low voices. Elizabeth was unsure whether to knock, clear her throat, or simply walk in.

As she debated whether to push the door fully open, she caught a glimpse of Adam handing something to Mr. Betterman, who quickly shoved the object under his loose-fitting jogging jacket. The hushed voices and quick action told Elizabeth that she wasn't supposed to be seeing what she was seeing. She turned to walk away, but accidentally banged the four-wheel cart against the wall, rattling the jugs and glasses. The two men spun around to face her.

"Sorry to interrupt, gentlemen," she stammered nervously, "but Mrs. Kottler asked me to bring some fresh water."

Adam looked particularly suspicious. "I don't need fresh water," he growled.

"I'm sorry," Elizabeth said again and retreated back into the hallway. With shaking hands, she grabbed the handle on the cart. *Why am I so nervous? What was that about?*

She heard a soft whirring behind her. Seconds later, Mr. Betterman navigated his electric wheelchair past her, pausing to look up at her through the black circles of his sunglasses. *I know who you are*, she expected him to say again. But he didn't say a word. He simply rode away down the hallway.

Elizabeth closed her eyes, trying to calm the fear that gripped her. A heavy hand fell on her shoulder, and she cried out, nearly jumping out of her skin.

"Whoa, now, calm down," Sheriff Hounslow said. "I didn't mean to scare you."

"I'm a little jumpy," Elizabeth admitted quickly.

"I guess you are. Is everything all right?"

"Yeah," she said. "First-day jitters."

"I thought yesterday was your first day."

"It was. But that was a tour. Today is my first day of *work*. Excuse me," she said and walked briskly away with the cart. Before she rounded the next corner, she heard the sheriff greet his father. Adam Hounslow launched the first assault by complaining about his room.

Safely down the next hallway, Elizabeth stopped again to take a deep breath. *This is stupid*, she told herself. *There's nothing to be afraid of. It was just two old men talking.* She scolded herself for being so easily freaked out and, after a moment, continued her rounds.

The rooms — *apartments*, as Mrs. Kottler called them — varied in appearance. A few looked like sterile hospital rooms. Others reflected attempts by the residents or their families to liven them up with furniture, family pictures and personal mementos. If awards were given for the homiest room, Frieda Schultz would win hands down.

From the moment Elizabeth stepped into Frieda's room, she felt transported out of the retirement center into a cozy bungalow. The room was colorful, with bright floral curtains and lampshades, and the smell of an air freshener that made her think of purple flowers. A chaise lounge had been placed in the corner, smothered with pillows that Frieda had probably made herself, Elizabeth guessed, and draped with a quilt that looked older than the residents at the center. The windowsill was covered with cards, fashion magazines, catalogs, and books by authors with names like Baroness Orczy and Georgette Heyer and Elswyth Thane — writers Elizabeth had never heard of. Victorian tapestries did their best to hide the institutional-white walls. An oak wardrobe with elaborately carved edging along the top and bottom replaced the plain, pressed-wood box the center provided. The matching bureau and vanity table, squeezed in along the opposite wall, were overrun with costume jewelry, evening purses, scarves, gloves, perfume bottles, jars, cold cream, tubes, a magnifying mirror, boxes, silver combs, and brushes. It gave Elizabeth the impression that Frieda might suddenly decide to call for her chauffeur and go out to the theater for the evening.

"I know, I know, it's a cluttered mess," Frieda said from the bathroom door in the corner.

Elizabeth realized she'd been standing in the middle of the room, staring. "I think it's wonderful," she said.

"Well, aren't you kind to say so." Frieda, a heavyset woman in a silk housecoat, sashayed into the room as if she were dressed in chiffon and lace and making a grand entrance at a formal ball. Her beauty had faded with age, but she exuded a poise and charm that hadn't. "Tell me your name, child."

"I'm Elizabeth. I'm here to give you some fresh water."

"A new volunteer?"

Elizabeth nodded as she flipped open the top on the copper-colored jug. Empty. She retrieved the large pitcher from the cart and poured water from one to the other.

"You must be traumatized," Frieda said. "A pretty young girl like you thrown in with all these fossils. What in the world are you doing here?"

"I volunteered through my church."

"And are regretting it now, I'll bet." Frieda laughed.

Elizabeth answered with a guilty smile.

"If it's any consolation, I'm very happy to meet you," said Frieda. "I get so tired of old people. And you're a churchgoer too. All the better. I'd go to church if it weren't such a major production to do so."

Elizabeth was surprised. "Production? Why is it a production?"

"I'm not about to bore you with my health problems. We have a chapel here that I can pray in. That'll do for now." Frieda pushed aside some of the pillows on the chaise lounge. "Put down those water jugs and come sit."

"But Mrs. Kottler wants me to — "

"Forget Mrs. Kottler," Frieda said. "I want you to sit down right here and tell me all about yourself. I don't get to meet new people very often and, when I do, I want to know their stories."

Elizabeth shyly sat down on the lounge.

Frieda placed herself on the opposite end, leaned back, and tucked one leg under her large frame. "Comfy? Good. Now ... tell me all about you."

Elizabeth began slowly with a few basic facts about growing up in Fawlt Line, her parents, her school. Soon, she was chatting away as if she had known Frieda forever. Any lull, any missing pieces, any evasion, and Frieda asked just the right question to set it straight and keep the conversation going. Elizabeth surprised herself by talking about her personal life: how her friendship with Jeff had eventually led to their dating relationship.

"Do you love him?" Frieda asked.

"Yes, I do," Elizabeth admitted, blushing.

"Childhood sweethearts," Frieda mused. "My Alexander and I were childhood sweethearts. We were married for forty-seven years. It wasn't always bliss, but I wouldn't have wanted to spend that time with anyone else."

They continued to talk for another half hour, until Elizabeth suddenly realized the time.

Elizabeth glanced at her watch and stood up quickly. "Oh! I've been here too long. Mrs. Kottler will be looking for me."

"Wait," Frieda said and placed a soft hand on Elizabeth's arm. "There's something you haven't told me." Her gaze was penetrating.

"What do you mean?" Elizabeth asked feebly.

"I have a sense about these things — a *gift*, in a way. There's something you haven't told me. You're holding something back."

Elizabeth glanced away nervously. Frieda was right: Elizabeth hadn't mentioned her time-travel nightmare. Having made a friend in the center, she wasn't eager to lose her by talking like a lunatic. "Yeah, but it's too crazy. I can't talk about it now. Maybe some other time."

Frieda watched her for a moment, then decided to let the subject drop. "All right. We have time. Other days, other talks, and maybe you'll tell me about it. I feel that somehow you *should* tell me. Maybe there are secrets I can tell you too."

Elizabeth felt such an instant rapport with the older woman that she was tempted to take her up on her invitation and pour out the whole tale on the spot. As she began to sit down again, Mrs. Kottler appeared in the doorway.

"There you are, Elizabeth!" she exclaimed. "I've been wondering what became of you. I need your help in the recreation room. There aren't enough judges for the Twister contest!"

○ ○ ○

Frieda insisted that Elizabeth could go only if she escorted Frieda into the recreation room. "My ankles are hurting today," she complained and sat down in a wheelchair that was folded up behind the door.

Elizabeth happily grabbed the wheelchair, clicked it into place, and whisked Frieda away, the smell of perfume trailing back to her.

"What's wrong with your ankles?" she asked as she pushed Frieda down the hall.

"I have occasional bouts with arthritis. Not today, actually, but I didn't want to let you go yet," Frieda replied.

The recreation room was filled with residents, many of whom Elizabeth had seen on her rounds. They sat at the card tables, on the sofas and chairs, engaged in different games and hobbies. At the opposite end of the room, Elizabeth saw Doug Hall in earnest conversation with Mr. Betterman.

"Oh," she said, without meaning to.

Frieda followed Elizabeth's gaze over to the two men. "I see," she said with a smile. "Handsome, isn't he, that young man? But watch out for him."

"Don't worry. I'm with Jeff, remember?" she reminded her newfound friend.

"Of course you are. But one can't help but notice Doug," Frieda said. "I'm sure he's already flirted with you. No pretty girl goes through here without him pouring on the charm."

"I talked to him for a minute yesterday."

Frieda smiled. "Uh-huh. It's nice, isn't it — having a handsome young man pay attention to you? Even if you know nothing will come of it."

"I guess."

"Just be certain that nothing *does* come of it, my dear," Frieda warned.

"What do you mean?"

"I know his type. He's a charmer, and the charmers are the ones who can hurt you the most."

Doug and Mr. Betterman parted, and Mr. Betterman wheeled himself out to the patio.

Elizabeth knelt closer to Frieda, and the woman's perfume lightly tickled her nose. "Do you know Mr. Betterman?" she asked.

Frieda folded her arms across her chest as if she were trying to contain a shiver. "As much as I care to," she said.

"You don't like him?"

"I don't know him well enough to like or dislike him."

"You're evading my question," Elizabeth teased her.

"I don't know him," she said carefully, "but I know my impressions."

"What're your impressions?"

She thought for a moment. "How can I put it in terms you'll understand? He gives me the creeps. There's something about him that seems ..." Her voice trailed off.

Elizabeth waited. When Frieda didn't continue, Elizabeth pressed her. "Seems what?"

"Evil."

4

Elizabeth relaxed in the bathtub, warm water up to her chin. She lifted up her right foot just as a drop of water fell from the tap and splashed cold against her skin. She sighed and closed her eyes, feeling her worries of the day seeping away into the warmth surrounding her. She wondered what Frieda was doing and smiled as she thought of how the older woman would approve of the luxurious bath Elizabeth was indulging in now.

Wait a minute! Elizabeth suddenly shot up in the tub. How did I get in this bathtub? I had already gone to bed. I know I had. I got home from the center, ate dinner, talked to Jeff on the phone, spent time with mom and dad and went to bed. Didn't I? Am I going crazy?

Instantly, she felt rough hands grab her, hard fingers wrapping around her throat, pressing tightly, pushing her under icy water.

Alarmed, Elizabeth grabbed at her throat, but couldn't lessen the strong grip. She couldn't see a thing as she gasped and struggled. She shouldn't be in the bathtub; and the water certainly shouldn't be this cold. But here she was, just like the night she'd slipped through the time fault and ended up almost being killed. Something had grabbed her throat then too, and she had ended up in another time, another place. Now, it was happening again.

"Please, God, help me," she prayed desperately.

Suddenly, the hands around her neck were gone, and Elizabeth coughed and sputtered, pulling in ragged breaths, trying to still her racing heart. She looked around the bathroom but saw nothing out of the ordinary. Then she glanced down into the bath and recoiled, jerking her legs up.

The water was filthy brown with bits of grass and sludge floating on top, as if a sewer backed up through the drain. Her stomach turned, and she grabbed the sides of the tub to pull herself out. She pushed but couldn't get her footing on the slick porcelain. Her legs splayed out and she lost her grip, sending her body splashing downward, sliding toward the front of the tub. She felt her head being pushed under the water, hitting the bottom. She thrashed out, her hands clawing at something, anything.

Who was doing this to her? And why? She wasn't going to give up without a fight.

She grabbed the edge of the tub, pulling herself up with all her strength, and catapulted over the side. The water spilled with her as she struck the cold tile floor. She curled up on her side, coughing and sputtering. She wanted to scream, but couldn't find the breath to do it.

Her mind raced, trying to make some sense out of what was happening to her, even as she feared the hands might somehow reach up from the depths and grab her again. It couldn't be happening again. Not like this. Not in the exact same way. Could it?

On unsteady legs Elizabeth stood — panic squeezing a cold hand on her heart. She'd fallen through time again. Somehow, she just knew it. She was in another Fawlt Line, where no one knew her, where they would think she was out of her mind, where someone obviously wanted to kill her. It was her worst nightmare all over again.

Elizabeth threw open the door to her bedroom and stumbled in, light spilling in from the bathroom. Everything was silent except for the sound of her own quickened breathing. Then she heard it. The soft whir of an electric wheelchair. It was coming toward her ... closer ... closer...

"I know who you are," a soft voice whispered.

Elizabeth screamed.

A flash of light pulled her out of her nightmare and into the arms of her mother. Jane Forde sat on the edge of the bed and wrapped her daughter in her arms. "It's all right," she said softly. "It's all right."

Elizabeth buried her face in her mother's neck.

After a moment, Mrs. Forde relaxed her grip, and Elizabeth pulled away and sat up. Her mother handed her a tissue for her wet eyes and dripping nose. "Can you talk about it?" she asked gently.

Elizabeth took a deep, nervous breath. "I was in the bathtub, and I couldn't figure out how I got in there, because I knew I had already gone to bed. Mom, a hand grabbed my throat, just like before. I think I was in that other time again."

Her mother frowned. "Oh, honey."

"I fought back and somehow got away over the edge of the tub. When I came out, everything was dark. Then I heard it — the wheelchair. And I saw him. Mr. Betterman, the man from the center that I told you about at dinner. He sounded so, so *sinister.* It was awful."

"I'm sure it was."

"I don't know what's wrong with me," she said as she rested her elbows on her knees.

Mrs. Forde clicked her tongue. "There's nothing wrong with you. You're wrung out, that's all. It's understandable. Mr. Betterman makes you uneasy, so he was still on your mind when you went to bed. I'm not surprised you had a dream about him."

"He spoke to me again. He said he knows me." Elizabeth shivered.

Mrs. Forde placed a comforting hand on her daughter's,

rubbing the smooth knuckles. "He's probably a senile old man who doesn't realize what he's saying."

Elizabeth balled up her tissue. "I don't want to work there anymore."

"I don't blame you."

"You don't?" Elizabeth said, surprised.

"Of course not. It's a new job, and something has brought back all the memories about that other time. And Mr. Creepy-in-a-Wheelchair isn't helping matters."

Elizabeth smiled, grateful for her mom's understanding.

"Look, I know it's not the same," Mrs. Forde continued, "but I remember when I was a cashier in a grocery store. I used to have nightmares about long lines of customers stretching back for miles and, sure enough, someone brought something to the counter without a price tag. Or the sale was three for fifty-seven cents, and they only brought two. My manager kept pointing at his watch and saying I had to hurry because the store was closing in two minutes. Talk about nightmares! I'll take Mr. Creepy over those dreams any day."

Elizabeth laughed, and Mrs. Forde took her hand. "Quitting or not is your decision. But I hope you won't let a nightmare make the decision for you. Give it one more day, just to see what happens."

Elizabeth thought for a moment. One more day. It was a fair proposition. "Okay."

Her mother kissed her on the cheek, and Elizabeth lay back in her bed.

Tucking her in, Mrs. Forde said, "To this day, I don't understand how we almost lost you to that other time. Your father tries to explain it, but I'm too simpleminded."

"You're not simpleminded, Mom. And even Dad is only guessing. Nobody really knows how it happened. Not even Malcolm. He says some things are too big for us to fully understand."

"All I know is that I lost you and then I got you back. For that,

I will thank God every day as long as I have breath to do it." She kissed her daughter again.

"Good-night, Mom."

"Good-night." Mrs. Forde floated out of the room on the wings of her housecoat.

Elizabeth lay on her back, staring at the shaft of light that stretched across her ceiling from the hallway. It reminded her of a golden sword.

I lost you and then I got you back. For that, I thank God, her mother had said.

God, don't ever let me get lost like that again, Elizabeth whispered, a fervent "amen" to her mother's statement.

She drifted to sleep as a storm rolled in.

5

Elizabeth was called to Mrs. Kottler's office as soon as she walked into the retirement center the next afternoon.

"Is something wrong?" she asked Mrs. Spriggins, the purple-haired woman who sat guard at the small wooden desk in the reception area.

"It's the storm," she answered, gesturing to the rain outside. "Something always happens when it rains like this. Two weeks ago it rained and rained, and Grace Peckinpah broke her hip."

Elizabeth didn't understand the connection between the rain, Grace Peckinpah's hip, and Mrs. Kottler's summons. But figuring that she wouldn't find out from Mrs. Spriggins, she walked through the small outer office to Mrs. Kottler's door. The voices on the other side were loud and unmistakable.

"We'll check into it, I promise," Mrs. Kottler said.

"*Who'll* check into it?" Sheriff Hounslow demanded. "Are you telling me you have an investigator on staff?"

"Well, no," Mrs. Kottler stammered. "We'll notify the police."

"I *am* the police!" the sheriff cried.

"Richard, calm down," Adam Hounslow said irritably. "Let me handle this, Dad."

"I know what you're thinking," Mrs. Kottler began. "But, Sheriff, they probably weren't stolen at all. Sometimes things are accidentally misplaced."

"She's right. I just forgot where I put them," Adam growled.

"That's nonsense, and you know it, Dad. You're not some senile crackpot — "

"Not yet, but maybe I'm becoming one."

Elizabeth suddenly realized that she was eavesdropping. Glancing back at Mrs. Spriggins, who peered at her over horn-rimmed reading glasses, she knocked softly on the door.

"Come in," Mrs. Kottler said, and looked visibly relieved when Elizabeth opened the door. "Oh, Elizabeth. I'm so glad you're here."

"Hi," Elizabeth said with a half smile. Mrs. Kottler and Sheriff Hounslow were standing in the center of the office. Adam Hounslow sat on the guest sofa nearby.

"When you were making the rounds with the water yesterday, did you happen to notice a gold ring and an old-fashioned shaving kit, or a framed black-and-white photo of the Hounslows in anyone else's room?" Mrs. Kottler asked.

"No, ma'am."

"Did you see them on the nightstand in my father's room?" Sheriff Hounslow cut in.

"I didn't go into your father's room."

The sheriff frowned. "I saw you there with your tray, remember? You jumped like you'd seen a ghost."

"But I never went in. I — "

Adam waved a hand at the sheriff. "Leave the poor girl alone."

"Sheriff, I can assure you that our staff, residents, and *volunteers* are above reproach," Mrs. Kottler said, glancing at Elizabeth.

"I'm only pointing out that she looked awfully nervous for someone who was just delivering water," Hounslow said in an accusing tone.

"It was her first day on the job," Mrs. Kottler said. "Volunteers are typically nervous. They're not used to everything yet."

Elizabeth was grateful for her intercession.

The sheriff folded his arms, which somehow made him look even bigger than he was. "Look, Mrs. Kottler, I don't care if these things were accidentally misplaced, stolen, or carried away by fairies in the night. I want them found. These are treasures. My mother gave my dad that ring, and the shaving kit was handed down from his father. The photo was his wedding picture."

"Were they your treasures or mine?" Adam demanded. "Why are you making such a fuss about *my* things?"

"Because they were valuable!"

Adam's voice was unmistakably mocking. "But they were just *things*, Richard. *Things*. And if there's one thing you've taught me, it's that *things* don't last. Like my house."

"Here we go again."

"Was my house misplaced? No, it was stolen from me. Stolen by my own son so he could hide me away in this expensive crypt." Adam sank into the sofa with a grunt.

"Stop it!" the sheriff snapped, then turned to Mrs. Kottler. "Maybe I should do a room-by-room search."

Mrs. Kottler shook her head. "That would be terribly stressful for our residents."

"Then what am I supposed to do?"

She spread her hands in appeal. "Let us handle it, Sheriff. We'll look for the missing items as we do our rounds. They're bound to turn up."

"Sure they will," he said skeptically.

"Quit being such a pompous pain in the neck!" Adam snarled at his son. "If you're in the mood to investigate, why don't you investigate what went wrong with our relationship, huh?"

"That'll be all, Elizabeth. You can go," Mrs. Kottler said with a weary expression.

Elizabeth left Mrs. Kotter's office, pulling the door closed on the two men arguing behind her. She nodded at Mrs. Spriggins and went out the reception room door. In the lobby she saw Mr.

Betterman whispering to another older man in a wheelchair. They stopped as soon as they saw her.

"Good afternoon," she squeaked awkwardly.

The other man waved from his chair. "Afternoon."

Mr. Betterman simply nodded.

Without betraying her desire to run down the hall away from the man who had haunted her dreams, Elizabeth picked up her pace and walked quickly away. She'd have given anything to walk out the front door at that moment and never come back, but she'd promised her mother — and herself — that she'd give it one more day. Maybe a visit with Frieda Schultz would cheer her up.

Frieda's door was open, so Elizabeth peeked in. She was leaning back in her bed, propped up against a mountain of pillows. She looked pale and tired, and was staring at a pot of pink bell-shaped flowers on the stand next to her.

"Hello, Mrs. Schultz," Elizabeth said as she entered the room.

Frieda jumped. "What do you want?" she cried out before she realized who it was. "Oh, I'm sorry. I didn't know it was you."

"I didn't mean to scare you." Elizabeth smiled.

"Scare me? Ha!" Frieda replied with forced humor. "I thought we scared you. I didn't think you'd come back."

Elizabeth was struck by Frieda's worried expression. "Maybe today will be my last day. Unless you can talk me into staying," Elizabeth said playfully.

"I wouldn't try," Frieda said with an unusually serious tone in her voice. "You're young. You should be with the young. Go away from here and don't look back."

Elizabeth stared at her. "What does that mean?"

"Did you happen to bring me some water today? My flowers need fresh water," she said, ignoring the question.

"I can get you some," Elizabeth offered and went into the

bathroom to fill a glass. "Why are you in bed? Aren't you feeling well?"

"I'm a little tired. And my ankles … you know."

"I thought you said your ankles were just an excuse." Elizabeth returned with a glass of water and came around the bed.

"Not today. Today I need to stay in bed. Just pour it around the edges. Yes, yes, like that. Don't get water on the leaves. Thank you."

"That plant is beautiful. What is it?"

"Don't you know? It's a gloxinia."

"I've never heard of it," Elizabeth said. "My dad loves to work in the garden. Maybe he'll grow some for me."

"Hand me that pad of paper — there, on the dresser — and I'll write the name down for you."

Elizabeth handed her the memo pad and a pen that bore the title *Courtesy of Fawlt Line Bank*. Frieda's hand trembled slightly as she wrote. Elizabeth adjusted the pot on the table, pushing aside the small medicine bottle and reading glasses next to it. Then she picked up the brown prescription bottle. "What're these for?"

"My ankles." Frieda shoved the piece of paper into Elizabeth's uniform pocket. "That'll tell you what you need to know about those flowers."

At that moment, Elizabeth looked Frieda fully in the eyes. The older woman's expression seemed desperate, as if she were trying to communicate something her words weren't saying.

"Mrs. Schultz — "

"Be careful," the old woman whispered.

Elizabeth looked at her quizzically.

"Shhh. It isn't safe. Don't talk." Frieda waved a hand at her as Doug appeared in the doorway.

"My two favorite ladies!" he exclaimed as he walked in. "I knew I'd find you together. Beauty attracts beauty, I always figure."

Elizabeth blushed, and Frieda waved a finger at him. "You're the kind of boy my mother warned me about," she said lightly, but there was no playfulness in her tone.

"Your mother would have loved me," Doug said with a grin.

Frieda sighed. "Yes, she probably would have."

Doug looked at Elizabeth. "Mrs. Kottler wants you for sheet detail."

"Sheet detail?"

"Uh-huh. You take the clean sheets from the laundry room and stack them in the various linen closets," he said. "Exciting, huh? I'd rather have you help me in the hot tub, but Mrs. K won't cooperate. How about you, Frieda? Care for some splashing around in the hot tub?"

"It's raining," she said, smiling wearily. "We'd get wet."

"That's the point," he said, and with a flirtatious wiggle of his eyebrows he left as suddenly as he'd arrived.

Elizabeth leaned closer to Frieda. "I'll stop by after I finish sheet detail. I want to ask your advice about something."

Frieda nodded.

"Meanwhile, get some rest."

"I think I'll skip the evening recreation time." The older woman gestured to a book on the table. "It'll give me a chance to catch up on my reading."

"Why did you say to be careful?" Elizabeth whispered.

Frieda's eyes darted quickly to the door, and she shook her head. "No, not now. Later. Come back."

○ ○ ○

Many of the residents were making their way to the recreation room as Elizabeth wove her way past them to the laundry room. A cart piled high with cleaned and folded sheets waited for her.

A short, dark-haired woman stood by the machines at the other end of the room. "Are you the new volunteer?"

"Yes, I'm Elizabeth."

"Terrific," the woman said without meaning it. "I'm Carmel.

I'm in charge of the laundry. Now, there are three linen closets around the building. Divide these sheets equally among them, and put 'em *neatly* on the shelves."

"Yes, ma'am," Elizabeth said and, with a hard push, got the cart moving toward the door.

"And don't mix the pillowcases in between them!" the woman shouted. "You volunteers always get 'em mixed up."

"I won't, ma'am," Elizabeth called over her shoulder. She pushed the cart to the first linen closet she came to, around the corner from the recreation room. Music echoed down the hall. A concert? A dance? Both, she remembered. Mrs. Kottler had invited in a small ensemble that specialized in big band music. She had seen the announcement for it on the bulletin board. Elizabeth wished she could be there. She didn't know anything about big band music, but it had been a long time since the prom, when she was supposed to get to dance with Jeff but ran into the displaced King Arthur instead. Jeff hadn't been too sad about missing the dance. He didn't like to dance to *any* kind of music.

An image of herself and Doug dancing close together flitted across her mind. She suppressed it immediately. Why did her imagination keep flirting with him like that? She couldn't account for it, but she was going to keep trying to stop it. She knew she should be loyal to her boyfriend, even in her thoughts.

She pushed the cart into the linen closet and went about her chore of stacking the sheets in their appropriate places on the large metallic shelves. She was extra careful not to mix in any pillowcases. Ten minutes later, she was on her way to the second linen closet, and not long after that she was on her way to the third closet at the far end of the complex. The music and general commotion from the recreation room were now a distant and muted cacophony.

Elizabeth tried to pull the cart into the small enclosure, but it wouldn't fit. She pushed it back into the hallway. The closet door bumped into her as it tried to close automatically. Grumbling, she shoved it open again and grabbed a stack of sheets. She wasn't far from Frieda's room now. If she hurried and finished the sheet detail, she could visit her again before the recreation time was over.

She had just stepped halfway into the closet to unload the stack of sheets, when she heard a familiar sound and froze. Could it be? *Yes.* It was the whirring of an electric motor on a wheelchair. The door thumped her from behind again, and the whirring sound came closer. Elizabeth's heart raced. She didn't want to see Mr. Betterman, and especially didn't want to have an encounter with him in a deserted part of the building. She didn't care if her fear was irrational. She didn't care if she had no legitimate reason not to like the man. She moved out of the door's path and allowed it to close, holding the handle so it wouldn't make any noise. Clutching the sheets to her chest, she waited.

The whirring got louder and louder until it was just outside the door. It slowed. Elizabeth lowered her chin and pressed her mouth against the sheets. *Was he right outside the door? Was it even Mr. Betterman at all?* She held her breath. Time seemed to stop. Then the whirring geared up again and faded away in the opposite direction down the hall.

Elizabeth exhaled long and hard, her heart banging against her rib cage. She tossed the sheets onto the shelf — still careful not to mix them with the pillowcases — and reached for the closet door handle.

It wouldn't turn.

She turned it once, twice, then pulled on it over and over until her arms and shoulders ached. The door wouldn't budge.

She was locked in.

6

Elizabeth stood still, her quick breaths the only sound she could hear. Then she renewed her attack on the door handle — and then on the door itself, pounding and shouting in the hope that someone wasn't in the recreation room and would hear her. The wheelchair she'd heard was long gone by now. How long before someone else would come by? Would anyone notice that she was missing? Doug Hall might, if he ran out of other people to flirt with. Maybe Mrs. Kottler would. But today was the big band concert, and the program would surely go longer than usual.

She leaned against the door and tried to control the panic that threatened to grip her. There was nothing to be afraid of, she told herself. Just sit down and wait until everyone returned from the concert. How long could it really be? An hour, tops? If she had a book she wouldn't complain. It was an hour of her volunteer obligation spent relaxing.

But she couldn't relax. She paced back and forth in the tiny cell. What if they didn't come back for two hours, or even three? What if there were a fire? What if ... what if this was another time fault and, when she stepped through that door, she found herself in another Fawlt Line once again?

Elizabeth swallowed hard. Was it hot in here? Why was she sweating so much?

"Calm down," she said aloud. "You're being really childish,

Elizabeth. They'll find you in no time at all. And you definitely don't want to look all freaked out when they do."

She dropped part of the stack of sheets onto the floor and sat down. *Make yourself at home. Be calm.*

Then the wailing started. It was soft at first but grew louder, a solitary, mournful sound in the hallway. *What was it?* Elizabeth had heard wind sound like that on cold winter nights. It was ghostlike, haunting. She stood up and rubbed her arms to keep her skin from crawling. The sound got louder. It was unmistakably human — someone was crying. Not in short sobs, but in a long howl. Where was it coming from? It wasn't in the hall, but coming from a small vent near the top of the wall. It went on and on.

She groaned and put her hands over her ears. *Somebody make it stop!*

She threw herself at the door again, pounding and shouting for help.

The wail stopped before she realized it. She listened to the silence, then sat down trembling, her nerves shot.

Suddenly, from beyond the closet door, another kind of commotion began. Heavy footsteps — a lot of them — were coming down the hallway. She heard the voices of men and women shouting. Elizabeth leapt to her feet again and renewed her assault on the door, praying she'd get someone's attention.

Someone jiggled the door handle.

"It's stuck!" she called out. "Can you hear me?"

Something very large was thrown against the door again and again. Elizabeth stepped as far back as possible. The door was defiant at first, then splintered and wrenched free as Doug Hall crashed through.

"Doug!" Elizabeth cried and fell into his arms with a sob.

"It's all right," he said soothingly. "That blasted lock gets jammed sometimes. We should have warned you."

With strong hands he grabbed her by the shoulders and looked straight into her eyes. "Are you all right?" he asked.

"I'm sorry. I'm a big baby," she mumbled.

"Don't worry about it." He guided her out of the closet with his arm around her shoulder.

She then noticed that some from the medical staff were gathered in a doorway farther down the hall. "Did something happen?"

Doug removed his arm and turned to face her, his face serious. "We had an emergency."

"What's wrong?"

"Frieda Schultz had a heart attack."

7

Elizabeth was no stranger to the idea of death. She had come face-to-face with it when she went through the time fault, and like many teenagers, she had lost a distant relative and attended a couple of funerals. The worst had been the memorial service for Jeff's parents, but she'd been little then, only ten. Still, none of those things had prepared her for the overwhelming loss she felt when Frieda Schultz died.

She slumped against the wall and sobbed, the shock of Frieda's sudden death too much on top of her trauma from being locked in the closet. A moment later, Doug's strong hands were guiding her again, this time to a cozy gathering of chairs at the end of the hall. Elizabeth didn't resist, even when he sat her down and put his arm around her.

His face was close to hers when he finally spoke. "It's terrible. The poor, old girl. She couldn't reach her buzzer to let anyone know."

Elizabeth suddenly remembered the noise. "Oh, Doug! I think I heard her when I was in the closet. I heard a terrible wailing. If I could have gotten out, maybe I could have helped her." She broke down again.

"You couldn't have done anything for her," he assured her. "Don't torture yourself. Her heart was bad — did you know that?"

Elizabeth shook her head.

"She didn't like to talk about it. I think she diverted attention from her heart by blaming her ankles or her toes or something."

"Her ankles. She said she had bad ankles." Elizabeth sniffled.

"That's it. There was nothing wrong with her ankles." Doug sighed. "I guess she'd left her heart pills in the bathroom. But why would she do that? She was supposed to keep them next to her bed."

Elizabeth was too grief-stricken to focus on what he was saying.

Doug sat silently, then looked at her and said, "I'm going to miss her. Frieda was one of the best things about this place ... until you came along."

Elizabeth glanced at him. She opened her mouth to speak, but his compliment moved her, and she started to cry again.

He held her close now, gently patting her back. "That's it. Just let it all out. You've had a tough time."

"I hate it here. I never want to come back again," Elizabeth sobbed.

"I feel that way too, most of the time," Doug said. "Maybe we should get out of here now. Go for a Coke or some ice cream. It'll take our minds off everything."

Elizabeth was tempted. It would be easy to rationalize leaving for a while, considering everything she'd been through lately.

Doug put a finger under her chin and tipped her face upward. "Let's go crazy and drive up to Hancock. That's where the fun is. I never hang around Fawlt Line unless I have to. How about it?"

"I can't. Jeff is picking me up tonight."

He dismissed the comment. "Call him and tell him you made other plans."

"I really can't," she answered. "But ... thanks for asking."

Doug put on an exaggerated pout. "Okay, I'll let you off this time. But only if you promise to go out with me another night."

Elizabeth wanted to say she couldn't because Jeff was her boyfriend. She wanted to say that she was only sixteen years old and probably too young for whatever Doug had in mind. But somehow the words wouldn't come. "We'll see," she said noncommittally.

Mrs. Kottler was in front of them before either realized it. "A tragedy," she said. "Doug, we're going to need your help with — " She paused to find the right words. " — certain details."

Doug stood up. "You've got it."

"You look awful, Elizabeth. I'm sorry this had to happen today, when you're so new at volunteering. But I can't have you wandering around depressing the residents. I think you should go home."

Mrs. Kottler raced away. Doug put a hand gently on Elizabeth's shoulder. "Just let me know if you need anything. I got an A-plus in comforting when I was in school."

She smiled gratefully at him, then got to her unsteady feet. The attendants wheeled a stretcher past her, the body of Mrs. Schultz outlined by the sheet that covered her. Elizabeth could smell her delicate perfume. She stood perfectly still, breathing it in until she could no longer detect even a trace of it.

Mr. Betterman sat alone at the far end of the hallway and watched the proceedings. Elizabeth wasn't certain, but she thought she saw the hint of a grin cross his lips.

8

That evening, the rain stopped and the skies cleared enough for the stars to peek through the clouds. Elizabeth and Jeff strolled hand in hand down the freshly paved sidewalks in the Historical Village. Malcolm had designed it to be as natural as possible, with grassy knolls and patches of trees.

Jeff had hoped a walk here would help lift Elizabeth's mood. She'd been very quiet since he'd picked her up at the center, but he didn't press to find out what was wrong. He knew she'd tell him when she was ready.

"Everything's on schedule for the Village to open," he said finally, just to break the silence.

Elizabeth didn't respond.

Undaunted, Jeff continued, "Malcolm finalized the deal on the Winchester Estate. It's a perfect replica of a — "

"I don't care, Jeff," Elizabeth said suddenly. "I just wish this Village would hurry up and open so we could talk about something else for a while."

Jeff was hurt, but he tried not to show it. "What else do you want to talk about?" he asked.

"Anything."

"Ummm . . . okay. You start."

She frowned. "I don't have anything to say."

"Something's on your mind, Bits."

"I have a *lot* on my mind," she growled.

"Like?"

"Like, why don't we ever go out? I don't mean down to the Fawlt Line Diner. I mean to Hancock or Grantsville? Just for a change. Don't you ever get tired of hanging out around here?"

Jeff was taken by surprise. "What's wrong, Bits? I mean, what's *really* wrong?"

"Nothing's wrong." She frowned. "Why does something have to be wrong for me to want to do something different?"

"Because the last time you talked like this was when you wanted to run away from home. Remember? Right before — "

She cut him off. "I don't want to talk about that."

They walked on in silence for a moment then veered down a solitary path. Jeff glanced at the signpost to be sure he knew where they were headed. "Did something happen at the retirement center?"

Elizabeth didn't answer at first, but then she took a deep breath. "Mrs. Schultz died of a heart attack."

"Mrs. Schultz? That woman you liked? Oh, Bits, I'm so sorry. That's terrible."

It all came pouring out. "I saw her a little while before she died. I knew something was wrong. She looked sick and was worried about something when she showed me her flowers."

Jeff cocked an eyebrow. "Worried about what?"

"I don't know. She told me to be careful. I was supposed to go back later to talk to her, but I got locked in the closet and that's when she died." Elizabeth shuddered and pressed herself closer to Jeff.

Jeff shook his head. "Locked in a closet? Good grief, what kind of day did you have?"

Elizabeth told him about the closet and the wailing she'd heard. "I was locked in that stupid closet while Mrs. Schultz was dying. And what makes it worse is that her pills were right there in the — "

She stopped and looked puzzled.

"What's wrong?" Jeff asked. "The pills were right where?"

"Wait a minute. That doesn't make sense."

In the dim light Jeff could see that Elizabeth's brow was furrowed in deep thought. "What doesn't make sense?" he asked.

"Her pills. They were on the table with the flowers. I saw them," she said, then thought about it more. "But Doug said that she couldn't get to them because she'd left them in the bathroom. That's not right."

"Are you sure?"

"Yes! They were right next to the flowers. How did they get into the bathroom?"

"Beats me." Jeff shrugged. "Maybe she took them in herself and forgot."

"Maybe," Elizabeth said, not believing it. "She may have carried them into the bathroom so she could take one with water. But there was water next to the bed. That doesn't make sense either. Would *you* carry your medication with you to another part of the room when you knew you'd need it right next to your bed?"

Jeff shrugged again. "I don't know. What are you saying?"

"Maybe somebody else moved them."

Jeff stopped on the path and turned to her. "Why would anybody do that?"

Elizabeth also stopped, hugging herself and frowning. "I don't know. But something's not right. I can't explain it, but I can feel it."

"Bits," Jeff said with a hint of impatience. "I'm not following you."

"Mr. Betterman," she said.

"The weird guy in the wheelchair?"

"He's the reason I got stuck in the closet. I heard him coming, and I didn't want him to see me, so I let the door close. That's when it got stuck."

"I still don't understand what that has to do with — "

"Don't you see? He was coming from Mrs. Schultz's room!"

Jeff turned to her. "Wait a minute. Are you saying Mr. Better-man took Mrs. Schultz's pills?"

"Maybe."

Jeff bit his lower lip. "But that's the same as saying he killed her."

Elizabeth nodded and continued to walk down the path.

Jeff followed. "You really think Mrs. Schultz was murdered? That's *huge*."

"I know!" Elizabeth cried out. "But nothing else makes sense. That creepy man keeps looking at me and giving me nightmares — "

"Nightmares?" Jeff asked, feeling more lost with every question he asked.

"Last night. I was going to quit the retirement center because of it. I dreamed that I was trapped in the other time again, and someone was choking me in the tub again. Then I walked into my room and *he* was there. For some reason, he reminds me of that other time. He brings back all the worst fears I have."

Jeff pulled her close. "The chances are almost nonexistent that you'll ever go back to that time. Malcolm said so."

"How does he know? Nobody knows. Freak coincidences happen all the time around here."

"So?" Jeff asked. "Remember what Crazy George said. 'Co-incidences are the secret workings of God.'"

"Yeah — and George is still stuck there!" Her voice was a shrill contrast to the peacefulness of the evening.

"Calm down, Bits. It's okay." Jeff pulled her close for a moment, then gently let her go.

"In a way, I wish I could go back through and save him," she said.

Jeff steered her toward a bench and they sat down. He softly moved a lock of hair from her face. "You have to put it out of your mind. You know how exact everything has to be on both sides of time for anyone to cross over. You and Sarah would have to be in the right places at the right times ... and the chances of that taking place a second time must be a trillion to one. It won't happen again. You're safe."

"But Crazy George is trapped."

"In a way I guess he is," Jeff said simply, but not without sympathy. "He's been there a long time. He has a life there now."

She glanced up and realized they were sitting across from the church ruin. It was the restored section of the church from England where King Arthur had slipped through a different time fault into the present. Next to the ruin, Malcolm had added majestic towers and vaulted ceilings.

"What about King Arthur?" Elizabeth asked.

"What about him?"

"Well, he didn't switch places with anyone. He just came through."

"He came through for a specific reason and — " Jeff didn't finish his sentence, but turned to her impatiently. "Look, I didn't say I had the answers for everything. All I know is what Malcolm says. Eternity is ... well, it's like a very large house and ... somewhere inside the house is a hallway that we call time. Maybe that hallway has different doors that are usually closed, but sometimes they slip open. Why they open and what happens when they do is anybody's guess. Only God knows for sure. All *I* know for sure is that we have our time right here and now, and we shouldn't waste it by worrying about things we don't understand."

She gazed at him, but he couldn't read her expression. Impulsively, he pulled her close and kissed her.

Embracing him, she whispered, "What am I going to do about the retirement center?"

"Do you want to quit?"

"Yes."

"Then quit. Tell them tomorrow. That way you can forget about that guy in the wheelchair and Mrs. Schultz and everyone else."

"What about Mrs. Schultz's pills?"

Jeff shrugged. "You could tell Sheriff Hounslow."

"He'd never believe me."

"Maybe not. But it won't hurt to try."

9

"Gone? What do you mean, she's gone?" Elizabeth asked.

Mrs. Kottler frowned sympathetically from behind her desk. "That's the procedure. She's examined to determine the cause of death, and then she'll be transported to her family in — " She flipped over a form on her desk to check her information. " — New York City."

"That's it? No funeral? I won't get to see her again?"

"I'm sorry. I didn't realize you'd become so fond of her," Mrs. Kottler said, rising from her chair and quickly moving around the desk.

"I thought I'd be able to say good-bye," Elizabeth said.

Mrs. Kottler patted Elizabeth's arm. "In your own way, I'm sure you still can."

Elizabeth sighed. There was no response to such a comment.

"I know what you're thinking," Mrs. Kottler said. "You're thinking that this will hurt the morale of the rest of the residents. But your friend Malcolm Dubbs has helped take care of that problem."

"He has?"

She smiled. "Oh yes! The whole building is abuzz. He has generously extended an offer for all the residents to come to the grand opening of the Historical Village — for free!"

"That's nice of him."

"Everyone is so delighted, and I can't say enough about his generosity! Even Adam Hounslow seems uncharacteristically pleased."

Elizabeth was glad, but then remembered Mrs. Schultz's pills. "Has the sheriff come in to see his father today?"

"Not yet. He doesn't usually arrive until later. Why?"

"I was just wondering."

Mrs. Kottler scrutinized Elizabeth carefully. "Are you all right? I'm sure what happened yesterday was a shock for you. Doug told me about your being locked in the closet. And then Mrs. Schultz dying. I'm certain you must be thinking about resigning."

"To be honest — "

"Oh, I hope you won't!" Mrs. Kottler exclaimed. "We're so desperate for help, and having young people around does wonders for our residents. You have no idea. You're all they've been talking about. The 'fresh-faced young girl,' they call you. Just seeing you makes them feel younger and more alive."

Except for Mrs. Schultz, Elizabeth thought bleakly.

"Doug Hall would be devastated if you left now." A knowing smile formed on Mrs. Kottler's face. "Please promise me that you won't make any decision based on what happened yesterday."

It suddenly occurred to Elizabeth that if some kind of foul play was responsible for Mrs. Schultz's death, maybe she could help expose it by sticking around. *But only if I can stay at opposite ends of the universe from Mr. Betterman*, she thought.

Elizabeth didn't promise anything to Mrs. Kottler, but she cautiously nodded her consent.

"Excellent!" Mrs. Kottler cried out and hugged Elizabeth gingerly, so as not to mess up their outfits. She briskly set about organizing Elizabeth's role in preparing the recreation room for the evening craft class. "Simply arrange the tables and chairs so that everyone can see the front clearly. Well, do the best you can. Most of them can't see anything anyway."

◌ ◌ ◌

Alone in the recreation room, Elizabeth began the tedious process of moving around chairs. Doug showed up a few minutes later and looked surprised to see her. "I just lost five dollars in the betting pool," he announced. "Everyone was putting money down on whether you'd be back. I see I didn't have enough faith in your strength of character."

Elizabeth blushed. "I would've bet against my coming back too," she confessed.

"Really?" He grabbed some chairs to help her rearrange the room. "Then why did you? You couldn't resist my good looks, right?"

She smiled. "Actually, it was Adam Hounslow's good looks."

"I should've known you were one of those women who like the old, wizened types." He scowled playfully, then his tone became softer. "So, when are we going out? My invitation stands."

"I'm only sixteen," she protested.

"So am I!" He was obviously lying. "We were made for each other."

Elizabeth rested her hands on one of the folding tables and looked at him nervously. "Look, Doug, I . . . I didn't say so yesterday, but . . . I have a boyfriend."

Doug feigned great shock. "You do?" he gasped.

"His name is Jeff. I think you'd like him."

"Impossible. I hate him," Doug said good-naturedly. In mock anger he pushed over a chair, and it crashed to the floor with a loud metallic clang.

"Everything all right in here?" Sheriff Hounslow asked from the doorway.

Startled, Elizabeth jumped, then put a hand over her mouth to stifle a giggle.

"Everything's fine, Sheriff," Doug said quickly as he scooped up the chair.

"I'm looking for Mrs. Kottler," the sheriff said sharply. "Do you know where she is?"

"No sir," Doug replied. Elizabeth shook her head to confirm it.

"I'll assume that, since we haven't heard otherwise, no one has found my father's belongings?"

Doug took a few steps toward the sheriff, presumably to keep from shouting their entire conversation. "I'm sorry, no. But we're sure they'll turn up."

"Uh-huh," the sheriff said and moved to leave.

"Sheriff," Elizabeth suddenly called out.

"Yeah?"

She opened her mouth to speak, but felt uncomfortable mentioning Frieda or the pills in front of Doug. "Are you taking your father to the Village for the grand opening Saturday?" she asked instead.

Hounslow grimaced. "I hadn't planned on it, but my dad seems to be excited about the idea. I can't imagine why." He walked off.

"Why did you people ever elect him sheriff?" Doug asked.

Elizabeth shrugged. "Don't look at me. I'm too young to vote."

❍ ❍ ❍

Later, during her evening break, Elizabeth stopped by Frieda's room. Someone had been busy. Most of Frieda's belongings were boxed up for shipping. The bed was stripped, the wardrobe doors stood open to reveal their emptiness, and all surfaces were bare except for the nightstand. Frieda's flowers still sat in their pot looking beautiful, oblivious to the loss of their owner. The room looked like any other hospital room now. Even the smell of perfume was gone.

Good-bye, Elizabeth thought. In the silence of the room, she remembered a phrase she'd heard at her Great-aunt Patricia's funeral: *Have mercy on your servant and commend her to everlasting peace.*

"Amen," she whispered aloud.

No sooner had she finished her prayer than she heard the whirring of the electric wheelchair. Elizabeth's ears were attuned to it now. She reacted quickly, moving around the bed and into the darkness of the bathroom, glancing warily at the door as she entered. If this one closed and locked her in, she might lose her mind.

She listened as the whirring of Betterman's wheelchair approached the room. *Please let him pass*, she prayed. But he didn't.

Mr. Betterman paused at the door, tipping his head ever so slightly this way and that in an almost mechanical way. Was he making sure the room was empty? Elizabeth put both hands over her mouth and tightened every muscle in her body to keep from moving — or shaking.

He guided the wheelchair past the bed and wove around the packed boxes.

What's he doing here? What does he want? Maybe he's checking for evidence, to make sure he didn't leave anything behind.

He came to the nightstand and looked at the flowers. Leaning forward, he pushed his nose into the bouquet and inhaled deeply.

Without meaning to, Elizabeth pressed back against the wall, nudging a metal ring that usually held a hand towel. It clicked loudly. Elizabeth's heart skipped a beat, and she stepped away, farther into the shadow.

Again Mr. Betterman tipped his head this way and that, then gently picked up the pot and put it on his lap. He grabbed the controls of his wheelchair and spun himself around. Elizabeth closed her eyes. Her mouth had gone dry. She desperately wanted to swallow, but feared the sound it might make.

The angle from the bathroom to the door gave her a clear view of him again — and him of her, if he happened to turn to look. She began to relax as he moved steadily toward the hallway.

Just before he reached the door, he stopped his wheelchair. He didn't look at her, but spoke anyway. "It'd be a shame for these flowers to die," he said. "I think it's a shame for *anyone* to die."

Elizabeth froze. She didn't breathe.

Then he did turn his head to face her. His black glasses reflected the fluorescent lights above in a way that made them look like lightning. "Wouldn't you agree, *Sarah*?"

O O O

"He called you *Sarah*?!" Jeff shouted. "He knew the name of your time twin?"

Malcolm waved at him impatiently. "Sit down and be quiet, Jeff. Can't you see she's upset enough?"

Elizabeth was sitting on the sofa in Malcolm's study. She'd called Jeff immediately to come pick her up at the center, but she didn't tell him what had happened until they were together with Malcolm.

Jeff sat down next to her. "I'm sorry, Bits. Maybe it's just a … a name of someone he knows … a coincidence."

"A coincidence?" Malcolm challenged him.

"Maybe," Jeff answered sheepishly. "How could he know? We never talked to anyone about what happened in the other Fawlt Line. Apart from Elizabeth's parents and us, nobody knows the whole story. Nobody else knows that the girl you swapped places with was named Sarah."

"Sheriff Hounslow knew," Malcolm remembered. "I told him."

"But he didn't believe you," Jeff replied. "And for Elizabeth's sake, he promised not to talk about it. The last thing any of us wanted was for tabloid reporters to come in and turn Fawlt Line into some kind of freak show. This Mr. Betterman *must* have made the name up, or has Elizabeth confused with someone he knows named Sarah."

"I'm not so sure." Malcolm tugged at his ear. "I wish I could figure out why his name seems so familiar to me. It's somewhere in the back of my mind." Malcolm shook his head, as if shrugging the mystery away. "I wonder what kind of game he's playing?"

"It's called the Let's-Scare-Elizabeth-to-Death game," Elizabeth answered shakily.

Jeff was relieved to see some color returning to her cheeks.

Malcolm paced for a moment with his hands folded behind his back — a sure sign that he was trying to work it all out in his head. "I suppose we could talk to him directly."

"He won't tell us anything." Elizabeth said.

"I wonder where he's from. Maybe Mrs. Kottler can tell us something." Malcolm shook his head. "No, asking her might draw too much attention to the situation. Hmm. What's the best way to proceed?"

"Then you believe me?" Elizabeth asked. "You think there's something weird going on at the retirement center?"

"I certainly do," said Malcolm. "There are too many odd connections not to believe you. This Sarah business clinches it."

"But *what* do you think is going on?" Jeff asked, bewildered.

Malcolm looked at Jeff helplessly. "In a million years, I couldn't guess. Not with this little bit of information. We'll have to watch and see."

"Watch and see?" Elizabeth asked. "Oh, no, I'm not going back. I can't. My volunteering days are over."

"You don't have to go back if you don't want to," Malcolm said. "You've done your time this week. Now you have a few days to relax and put it out of your mind."

"Not a chance."

"Maybe Betterman will come to the grand opening," Malcolm said hopefully. "I might get a chance to see him there."

"And then what?" Jeff asked.

"Then we'll play it as it comes."

10

Under blue skies and a hot sun, people came from all over for the grand opening of the Historical Village. At noon on Saturday, the mayor made a long speech congratulating Malcolm for his contributions to the local economy — as if that were the reason Malcolm built the Village — then, with a pair of gigantic gold scissors, he cut a long red ribbon that wound around the front gates. Someone on the city council read a telegram offering the best wishes of the governor. Red, white, blue, pink, purple, silver, and gold balloons were released all over the grounds and flew to the clouds like colorful geese.

The crowds poured in and, for a little while, the parking attendants and security guards were afraid they'd have to turn people away. Luke Goodwin, the fire marshal, twitched his thick gray mustache and kept a watchful eye. Reporters for newspapers and local television stations spread out and interviewed anyone they could persuade to stop and talk. Even a national news network showed up for five minutes with a reporter and a camera. Malcolm said it must've been a slow news day.

Jeff and Elizabeth strolled the grounds and tried to enjoy the Village with everyone else. It was easier for Elizabeth, in some ways, since she'd mostly steered clear of the chaos around the organization of the opening, as well as the church where King Arthur had appeared — just in case. Jeff, on the other hand, had helped where he could, doing everything from painting sites to coordinating the delivery of antiques. Now he glanced around anxiously, too aware of all the things they hadn't been able to finish. But the smile on his face told everyone that he was proud to be part of Malcolm's great accomplishment.

Near the mining row house display in the southwest corner of the Village, Elizabeth spotted some of the residents from the retirement center. Sheriff Hounslow walked past with his father, bickering as usual. Dolly Higgins, a little gnome of a woman with a bright smile and twinkling eyes, pinched Elizabeth on the cheek and called her the "fresh-faced young girl." Then she looked at Jeff and trilled, "Is this your *boyfriend*?"

"Yes, he is," Elizabeth replied.

Dolly looked Jeff up and down and said, "Oh, I could fancy one like him myself."

Jeff turned crimson, and Elizabeth laughed.

Elizabeth saw more of the center's residents and thought most of them had come. They wandered in groups of two or three, some with members of the staff or family. A few hobbled along with walkers, and some rode in wheelchairs or the carts Malcolm had provided for anyone who needed them. They stared like wide-eyed children at the nineteenth-century farmhouse, the Shakespearean-style cottage, the Dutch windmill, the church ruin, the cluster of schoolhouses that represented the development of education in the United States throughout the past three centuries, the 1920s gas station, the grocery stores . . .

As Elizabeth watched some of the residents gather around the twentieth-century displays, she imagined the memories they must have. "Do you remember that?" she heard someone say, and "Oh, we had one of those in our house" or "I used to play in a room like that." Some merely gazed on wistfully.

What were they thinking? she wondered. Did they long for a piece of their past, or wish for a time lost to them? Was it mere nostalgia, or did part of them desire to reclaim what was once theirs — their youth, their happiness, their missing loved ones?

"Look at them," Jeff said softly, and Elizabeth knew he was wondering the same thing. "They make the whole thing worthwhile. It's not just history to them. It's part of their lives."

A voice from behind them exclaimed, "Well, now, look at the happy couple."

Elizabeth and Jeff turned to find themselves face-to-face with Doug Hall.

"Doug!" Elizabeth said. "I didn't know you were coming."

"I wouldn't miss it." He smiled then stretched out a hand to Jeff. "You must be Jeff. Elizabeth's told me a lot about you."

Jeff shook his hand, undisguised suspicion on his face. "Funny, she didn't mention you at all."

"I'm her little secret at the retirement center." He winked. "I'll bet you thought she was volunteering for humanitarian reasons. Don't believe it."

"Doug rescued me from the closet," Elizabeth explained quickly.

"Oh — that was nice of you," Jeff said.

"I thought so too." An awkward silence followed, then he said, "Well, I better go. Mrs. Kottler asked me to play camp counselor for the kids today. Nice to meet you, Jeff." He darted off into a group of residents, and the ladies instantly began cooing over his arrival.

"So," Jeff said as nonchalantly as he could, "how many times has he asked you out?"

Elizabeth giggled and put her arm in his. "There's nothing to be jealous about."

"I'm not jealous."

"Good. You don't need to be," Elizabeth said. They walked together for a while, with residents stopping Elizabeth periodically to say hello. Finally, Elizabeth looked around and said, "I haven't seen Mr. Betterman."

"Maybe he decided not to come."

"Good."

At a fork in the path leading to the mining row houses in one direction and the Park 'n' Dine diner in the other, they bumped into Sheriff Hounslow again. He was standing in the middle of the crowd with his hand up to shade his brow, scanning the area.

"You haven't seen him, have you?" he asked them.

"Who?"

"My father," he snapped, as if it should have been obvious.

"No," Elizabeth said.

"You *lost* your dad, Sheriff?" Jeff teased. "How does a sheriff do that?"

The sheriff gave him a cold look. "We were going through the miners' houses when he sent me off to get him a drink." He brandished a cup of soda as if to prove his story. "When I got back, he was gone."

"Maybe you should go to the office or the lost-and-found," Jeff offered. "They have speakers set up throughout the Village so announcements for lost kids or lost parents can be made."

Preoccupied, the sheriff continued to look through the crowd. "It's confounding," he muttered as he walked away. "It's like he *wanted* to lose me."

"I've had the same feelings myself," Jeff said under his breath after Sheriff Hounslow had gone. Elizabeth tried not to giggle. They circled through the Village and made their way toward the front gate again. Both were surprised that it was already late afternoon. They stopped by the front office where Malcolm was giving directions to the parking supervisor via walkie-talkie.

After signing off, he said, "All in all, the day has been a success."

"A *huge* success, Malcolm," Elizabeth corrected him.

"No crises, no catastrophes."

Jeff held up a hand. "No, wait. You had one. Sheriff Hounslow's father disappeared."

"Really?" Malcolm said. "I haven't heard anything about that."

"Don't worry about it. He's bound to turn up," Elizabeth said.

Suddenly Mrs. Kottler was upon them. "There you are, Elizabeth. I was wondering when I would bump into you. Oh, hello again, Mr. Dubbs — "

"Malcolm."

"Malcolm, of course." Mrs. Kottler laughed. "And you're Jeff, I know. It's been a wonderful day so far, hasn't it? Thanks so much for allowing our residents to come. We're trying to get them back to the center now. You can imagine how tired they are. But — and I'm so embarrassed about this — we seem to have botched up our car pool. Dolly Higgins's family brought her, but they couldn't take her back, so we're one off. Anyway, Dolly needs a ride, and I'm absolutely desperate to come up with a way to get her back to the center without making another trip ..." She let her final sentence hang for a moment.

Jeff grabbed it. "Elizabeth and I would be happy to help. We can take Dolly back."

Mrs. Kottler clapped her hands excitedly. "Oh, would you? You're wonderful. Thank you. She's ready whenever you are. No rush. She's just outside on the bench. Thank you, thank you!" She left the office, her heavy perfume lingering behind her.

Elizabeth pinched Jeff's cheek. "You're wonderful as well as cute!"

They collected Dolly and walked slowly with her to Jeff's Volkswagen. As they wound their way through the parking lot, Elizabeth spotted Doug Hall also walking between rows of cars. She nearly called out to him until she realized he was pushing a wheelchair. In it was Mr. Betterman.

"That's him. That's Mr. Betterman," she whispered to Jeff out of Dolly's earshot.

Jeff glanced around quickly. "It looks like they're leaving. Malcolm will be disappointed that he missed him."

"I'm not."

They reached the edge of the employee parking area where Jeff had left his Beetle earlier in the day. Elizabeth crawled into the back so Dolly would have an easier time getting in. Dolly thanked them a dozen times for being so nice to her.

As they putted along to the retirement center, Elizabeth thought about Mr. Betterman and Doug again. *That's weird. Why was Doug* pushing *Mr. Betterman's electric wheelchair?*

Jeff waited in the car while Elizabeth walked Dolly to her room. Though it was still early evening, the hallways in the retirement center were fairly deserted.

"Everyone's worn out from such an exciting day," Dolly said when they reached her doorway. "I'm a mite tired myself."

"Me too."

"Thank you for the lift home, dear. Good-night." Dolly shuffled into her room.

Elizabeth waved good-night and walked back down the hall. She passed Adam Hounslow's room and remembered that he had disappeared earlier in the day. Maybe he got separated from his son and found a way back to his room somehow. She stopped to check, but the door was shut. It was unusual for the residents to close their doors, even when they were away. She knocked softly. No response. She knocked again and whispered, "Mr. Hounslow?" Still no response. She reached down and put her fingers on the door handle.

"What are you doing?" a voice echoed down the hall.

She jumped and turned. Mr. Betterman was at the end of the corridor. He put his wheelchair into gear and drove toward her. She wanted to run, but was afraid it would make her look guilty of something. "Sheriff Hounslow couldn't find his father at the Village, so I thought I'd check to see if he was here."

"He's not," Betterman said.

"Oh, okay." Elizabeth turned to leave.

"Sheriff Hounslow's a law enforcement officer. If he can't find his father, what makes you think you can?"

Elizabeth felt her face go red. "I didn't say I could find him. I just thought, since I was here, I'd peek in. That's all."

"Well, he's not, so don't worry your pretty little head about him ..." As if for dramatic effect, he added, "Sarah."

Elizabeth faced Betterman — taking in his trademark jogging outfit and shoes, the cap and beard and mustache, and the black sunglasses that wouldn't let her see his eyes. "Why do you call me Sarah?"

A flicker of a smile formed at the corners of his mouth. "It's your name, isn't it?"

"No," she said. "My name's Elizabeth."

"I'm sure that's what they keep telling you. But we know better, don't we?"

Every instinct in Elizabeth's body told her to get away and get away now. "I think you have me confused with someone else."

The tiny smile stayed frozen beneath his whiskers. "I'm sure I don't."

"I have to go," Elizabeth said abruptly and spun around to walk away.

"Go on. But we'll talk again soon," he said, then laughed.

His laughter was still ringing in her ears when she collapsed into the passenger seat of Jeff's Volkswagen.

"I didn't know you were going to tuck her in and read her a bedtime story," he said.

"Just drive," she snapped.

○ ○ ○

When Jeff heard about Elizabeth's encounter with Betterman, he thought it was worth driving back to the Village to tell Malcolm. The sun was falling when they arrived.

"Uh-oh. I wonder what's going on?" Jeff said.

Elizabeth looked over. Several police cars sat in the employee lot.

Jeff parked nearby and they walked through the front gate. One of Hounslow's officers stood guard and initially stepped forward as if to stop them. He relaxed when he realized who they were.

"What's going on?" Jeff asked him.

"The sheriff's father is missing. We're watching the gates while the staff searches the park."

Jeff and Elizabeth went straight to the office. It was in a state of chaos as stricken-looking staff buzzed around Malcolm and Sheriff Hounslow, waiting for orders. Spread in front of them on the desk was an array of blueprints.

"I'm telling you, we've turned this place upside down," Deputy Peterson, the sheriff's right-hand man, said. His uniform, badly fitted around his barrel-like body, was damp with sweat. He grabbed a handkerchief and wiped the beads of water off his bald head. "We can check again, but I don't think he's here."

"What's standard procedure in a case like this?" Malcolm asked.

Sheriff Hounslow was pacing nearby. "Standard procedure is to wait twenty-four hours before putting in a missing person's report."

Jeff nodded to Elizabeth. That's what he'd been told when she had vanished.

"We're talking about your *father*, Richard," Malcolm reminded him. "Pretend it's twenty-four hours later and tell us what we should be doing."

"We'd have to look at the various possibilities," Hounslow said and paused in his pacing to peer out the office window that overlooked the Village. "Maybe he had a heart attack and collapsed somewhere in the park."

"But we've already — " Deputy Peterson began.

Hounslow held up a hand. "I know, I know. He's not here. So we might consider that the heat of the day affected his mind and he wandered off."

"Has anyone checked the retirement center?" Malcolm asked.

"We were just there," Jeff interjected. "Elizabeth went inside and stopped by his room. They said he wasn't there."

"Who said?" Hounslow asked.

"Mr. Betterman," Elizabeth replied. With the mention of that name, Malcolm looked curiously at Elizabeth, then Jeff. Jeff nodded as if to say they needed to talk later.

"Don't know him. Bob, send someone out to make absolutely sure," the sheriff said.

"Already done," Peterson replied. "Mrs. Kottler is having her people check around."

"Okay, so we fan out from the park to see if he's wandered off in some kind of daze," Malcolm said.

"Yeah," the sheriff said wearily, rubbing the back of his neck. Deputy Peterson grabbed his cap and went out to see that it was done. With the exodus of Peterson and some of the staff, the office was left to Malcolm, the sheriff, Jeff, and Elizabeth.

Hounslow sat down heavily in a chair and spoke as if he'd been in the middle of a thought. "Unless he's been kidnapped ..."

"Do you think that's likely?" Malcolm asked, surprised.

"No, but I can't rule it out," Hounslow replied. "I'll tell you what's *likely*. He ran away."

"You're kidding."

Hounslow shook his head. "If I treated this like any other case, I'd have to consider it a possibility. He hated the retirement center. Maybe he came up with a way to escape."

"Escape to where? Does he have other relatives or friends?" Malcolm asked.

"No, which is why it's hard for me to imagine him actually

doing it. But as I said, I have to consider every possibility." Hounslow sighed.

The four of them waited in silence for a moment. Elizabeth wondered if now was the time to tell the sheriff about the strange things that had been happening at the retirement center. Maybe there was a connection between Frieda Schultz's death and his father's disappearance.

She was just mustering the courage to bring up the subject when Hounslow suddenly leapt to his feet. "I'm not waiting around here. I want to go back to that mining display."

"The row houses?"

"That's the last place I saw him. I might have a better chance of finding a clue now that most of the people have gone."

⚙ ⚙ ⚙

Sheriff Hounslow, Malcolm, Jeff, and Elizabeth walked into the small row house that represented the late 1920s. It had the kinds of things most homes would have: a small living room with a sofa, a chair, and a reading lamp sitting on a large worn rug. A coal-burning stove called a "Heatrola" sat in the corner. The walls had a few meager framed photos of stern-looking men and women in washed-out sepia tones.

"My father was the son of a miner," Hounslow said as he glanced around the room. "Houses like this were called 'company houses' by some, because the mining company owned them. The miners nicknamed them 'patches.' My father grew up in one just like it."

The kitchen was visible through an adjacent doorway. They crowded in. One wall was lined with a free-standing sink and coal oven range, a small wooden table, and several shelves stocked with Campbell's soups, Morton's salt, baking powder, Pillsbury flour, Jack Frost Cane Sugar, Ivory starch, and Borax soap. A bathtub with a wooden cover sat along another wall. Several hooks in the wall above it held a large coat, a black mining helmet with a lamp attached to the front, and a handheld lantern. A lunch pail sat on the floor next to a pair of old black shoes. Elizabeth was struck by the starkness of it all.

She knew that Malcolm had wanted to include the row houses to pay tribute to the many people who had worked the coal mines in Fawlt Line and surrounding towns in the first half of the twentieth century. Now the mines were closed, replaced by new technology and energy sources, but it was interesting to see how the miners lived then.

Hounslow continued, "My dad used to tell me how his father would come home with a face so black from the coal dust that all you could see were the whites of his eyes. He climbed into one of those old tubs, and the kids would take turns scrubbing the dirt from his back."

Malcolm walked over to a door on the opposite wall and jiggled the door handle.

"Does that go anywhere?" the sheriff asked.

"When we get to phase three or four of this Village, it may lead to a back garden. But for now there's a wall on the other side."

The four of them squeezed up the narrow flight of stairs and walked to the second floor.

"Did your dad work for the mines too?" Elizabeth asked.

Hounslow nodded. "Before I was born. But one night there was a cave-in and his mining partner was killed. He quit right then. Still, there was something about the mines that stayed in his soul. He talked about them a lot. I think that's why he wanted to see this display so badly. Do you have a company store?"

"Company store?" Jeff asked.

"Department stores for miners," Hounslow replied. "They sold everything from furniture and clothes to shoe polish and match-sticks. They were owned by the mining companies, which often took advantage of the miners. They would pay their workers with vouchers that could only be used in the company store, so the miners had no choice but to buy there — and pay twice what they would have paid at a regular store."

"That's not fair," Elizabeth said.

"It sure wasn't," Hounslow agreed, then pushed open a door on the right side of the upstairs hallway. "Should this be closed?"

"Probably not," Malcolm answered.

The door opened into a bedroom. It had a bed, dresser, wardrobe, and nightstand. Near the small window stood a wash table with a small mirror attached to the top. A washing bowl sat on the top center with various toiletries surrounding it.

Suddenly, Hounslow's face went pale, and he walked slowly over to the wash table. "Hey."

"What's wrong?" Malcolm asked.

Sitting at the back of the table was an old black-and-white photo of a man and woman on their wedding day. Next to the photo were an old shaving kit and a modest gold ring.

The sheriff turned and glared at Malcolm. "These were stolen from my father."

12

Donald Nelson, a meticulous man with a thin face and a body that seemed all angles, was in his office — a glass-enclosed cage in the corner of the Village's receiving warehouse. As the director of the Village's acquisitions, it was his responsibility to label and catalog every item placed in the Village, no matter how large or small. As a result, his desk and the surrounding floor looked like a time traveler's garage sale. There were items ranging from Victorian pen sets to cowboy boots, Napoleonic brooches to eighteenth-century baby cribs, colonial American wigs to Slavic milk wagons.

He peered over his horn-rimmed glasses as Malcolm, Sheriff Hounslow, Elizabeth, and Jeff hurried in. The glow of his desktop computer screen was reflected in his glasses and it gave a light-blue tint to the two patches of white hair that sprung from above his ears. "Hello, Malcolm," he said in a high-pitched voice. "What are you doing here? You should be out celebrating the success of your grand opening!"

"You should too, Donald," Malcolm replied then introduced everyone. "We're still trying to find the sheriff's father. You've heard about him?"

"Missing, right? Yes, some of the staff were in here searching an hour or so ago. It certainly puts a damper on the day."

Careful not to smudge any potential fingerprints on the

shaving kit, photo, or ring, the sheriff had put them into plastic
bags. He now held them up for Donald to look at. "Recognize
these?" he asked.

Donald laughed. "As well as I might recognize any of the other
thousands of items we have displayed here. No, Sheriff, I'm sorry.
But if you'd be so kind as to put them on the desk, I can look for
an identifying number and check it against our inventory on the
computer. We have complete purchasing histories of everything
here."

Hounslow obliged, and Donald looked the items over, hum-
ming as he did. "Very nice." He brought them closer to a red
lamp and scrutinized each one through a large magnifying glass.
"Your father's, were they?"

"Yeah."

"He took very good care of them," Donald said. "Even the ring
is barely scratched."

"Do you recognize them or not?"

Donald didn't seem to notice the sheriff's impatience. "There's
nothing on any of them that indicates they've been through our
system. No numbers, not even the infrared mark. However, even
my staff is fallible. Perhaps we missed them. I'll cross-reference
the items on the computer." He swung around to the keyboard
and hammered in the descriptions. The computer beeped a
couple of times then displayed the information.

"Well?" Hounslow asked.

Donald shook his head. "Very curious. They're not listed.
Where, exactly, did you find them?"

"In the 1920s mining row house," Malcolm answered.

"I'll check that as well," Donald said. A dozen clicks later, he
frowned. "They're not listed. Whoever brought them in didn't
check them through my office."

Malcolm turned to Hounslow. "Is it possible your father put
them there?"

"That's ridiculous," the sheriff replied. "Why would he do a thing like that?"

"Why would he disappear?" Malcolm asked in reply.

The radio on the sheriff's belt hissed to life with crackle and static. "Sheriff?"

Hounslow grabbed the radio. "Hounslow."

"Nick here, sir," a young voice said. "I'm at the retirement center and — well, you should probably come out here."

"Did you find my father?"

"Not really, but ..." The rookie didn't finish. "You just oughta come."

"I'll be right there." Hounslow signed off. He looked at Donald and struggled with his words. "I'm sorry to be so irritable, but you must understand how anxious I am to find out how my father's personal belongings got in that mining house."

Donald nodded gravely. "Sheriff, rest assured I'll keep digging. If there's anything I discover about your father's things, I'll let you know."

"Thank you." He jabbed a finger toward Malcolm. "We're not finished with this business." He marched off.

Malcolm, Jeff, and Elizabeth looked at each other quizzically.

"We're not just going to wait around here, are we?" Jeff asked.

"He disappeared in our Village," Malcolm said. "I suppose we're responsible to help solve this case."

Elizabeth listened, knowing that the two would do whatever it took to help find the sheriff's father. She couldn't shake the feeling that all the strange events she'd witnessed recently — Mr. Betterman calling her *Sarah*, the closet incident, Mrs. Schultz's death, Mr. Hounslow's belongings and now his disappearance — were somehow connected.

"We have the reputation of the Village to think about, if nothing else," Jeff suggested. "We wouldn't want its name tarnished."

"Then let's go," Malcolm said.

"Wait a minute, Malcolm," Donald called out, beckoning him over.

Malcolm looked back to Jeff and Elizabeth. "You two go on to the retirement center. I'll keep investigating here. Call me later."

Jeff nodded and took Elizabeth by the hand. They strode off through the warehouse to his Volkswagen.

⚙ ⚙ ⚙

Donald tapped his computer screen. "There's an entry here — completely mislabeled and misfiled. It looks like the sheriff's father's belongings. One gold ring ... here's the shaving kit and ... here's the wedding photo."

"Who entered it?" Malcolm asked.

"Miss Clark," Donald called out.

A pretty blonde-haired girl peeked out from between two large packing crates halfway across the warehouse. "Yes, sir?"

He gestured for her to come over. "Miss Clark is a history student who's been interning with us this summer," he explained to Malcolm.

Miss Clark, whose tanned athleticism and khaki outfit looked more appropriate for someone hiking a mountain than inventorying artifacts in a warehouse, arrived at Donald's desk.

"What's the meaning of this?" Donald asked and pointed to the screen.

She squinted at the list. "The meaning of what, sir?"

"This is sloppy work," Donald said without being unkind. "These items shouldn't be under a miscellaneous category."

She ran her fingers through her long hair. "I'm sorry. I assume that in the rush of the last few days, someone didn't take the time to catalog those items properly. I'd gladly take the blame, but — " she pointed to the date of the delivery " — I wasn't here that day."

Donald grunted and scrolled down the screen to find out where the delivery had come from. "Thank you, Miss Clark.

Please get the word around to the rest of the staff that I won't tolerate shabby procedures."

"Yes, sir," she said and quickly disappeared behind another crate.

"Any idea where they came from?" Malcolm asked.

Donald held up a finger. "Yes, according to the inventory list they came from Miller's Olde Antique store, here in Fawlt Line." He called the antique store, and Malcolm watched as Donald had a brief conversation, then hung up and turned back to him. "Its closed, but the owner's there. He'll wait twenty minutes for us to get there."

✿ ✿ ✿

At the retirement center, Mrs. Kottler stood in Mr. Hounslow's room, clearly beside herself. "Sheriff, I have no idea what happened here."

The sheriff was livid.

Jeff and Elizabeth positioned themselves across the hall, but could see into the room. Someone had cleaned it out completely. All that was left was the bed with its rolled-up mattress and the institutional nightstand and wardrobe.

"It looks as though he was never even here," Elizabeth whispered to Jeff.

"I didn't authorize anyone to touch his room," Mrs. Kottler said, her normal confidence shaken. "Honestly. This must be some sick person's idea of a practical joke."

"Or a robbery," Hounslow said. "But why just his room?" He spun around to the three officers who had been waiting anxiously nearby and pointed to the rookie who had originally called him on the radio. "You — search the grounds."

"Yes, sir," the officer said and ran off.

"You two go room by room and talk to the residents and staff," Hounslow said to the other officers. "Somebody has to know something. Those things didn't just walk out of here!"

"Be nice to my residents!" Mrs. Kottler called after the officers. "They're fragile!"

Hounslow glared at her. "Most of them are tough as nails. You don't have to worry."

Elizabeth thought back to earlier when she had escorted Dolly back to her room and seen Mr. Hounslow's closed door. She had just placed her hand on the doorknob when Mr. Betterman stopped her. Had he been trying to keep her from seeing that the room was empty? She tried to recall the exact details. Mr. Betterman in his wheelchair. The way he came down the hall toward her. There was something wrong with the way he looked. What was it?

Hounslow stepped into the room and surveyed it, hands on his hips. He stood rigid and tense, his mouth set in a grim straight line.

"How long does it take to recharge a battery on a wheelchair?" Elizabeth suddenly whispered to Jeff.

Jeff looked at her, surprised. "I have no idea."

"Doug Hall was pushing Mr. Betterman in his wheelchair at the Village. But when I saw him here just fifteen minutes later, it was running like always. Could he charge it that fast?"

"I doubt it."

Elizabeth was quiet for a moment. That was part of it but there was something else ... What was it that niggled at the back of her mind?

"Bits," Jeff said. "Maybe it's time you told the sheriff what you know."

13

"Let me get this straight," Hounslow said to Elizabeth once they were in Mrs. Kottler's office. "One of the residents gives you the creeps because he thinks he knows you from somewhere else, you have a nightmare about him, then you get stuck in a closet and Mrs. Schultz has a heart attack because you *think* someone moved her pills?"

Elizabeth frowned. She should have known he wouldn't listen. "She was afraid that night. She was acting really weird."

The sheriff leaned against Mrs. Kottler's desk and folded his arms. "Yeah, sure. And half the people in here will tell you she acted weird all the time. She was quite eccentric."

Jeff, who'd been standing quietly nearby, moved forward. "What about Mr. Betterman going into her room the next day?"

"What about it? He's a plant nut. He didn't want hers to go to waste, like he said. No offense, kids, but my father is missing, and I don't have time for your Sherlock Holmes routine." He stood up.

"Then how about Mr. Betterman stopping me outside your father's room earlier?" Elizabeth challenged him.

Hounslow puffed out his cheeks peevishly. "If you had opened the door and seen whether the room was empty at that time, it would be helpful to me. Otherwise, all you have are your impressions of a man in a wheelchair who, by your own admission, 'bothers' you."

Elizabeth sat down resignedly.

"What about the battery on the wheelchair?" Jeff asked, not ready to give up. "Why would Doug Hall be pushing him one minute at the Village, and the next minute Betterman's driving down the hallway?"

"Maybe he has a replacement battery. Maybe there were two different wheelchairs."

"He called me *Sarah*," Elizabeth snapped, bringing up the one thing she knew better than to mention. "That was the name of the girl I switched places with in time."

Hounslow glared at her. "Don't start with Malcolm's time-travel mumbo jumbo. I didn't believe it then, and I don't believe it now."

Jeff frowned. "So you're not even going to question Betterman?"

Hounslow growled, "Oh, I'll question him, all right. But not because of what you've told me."

There was a knock at the door, then Mrs. Kottler peeked in nervously. "Sheriff? They're calling for you. It sounds important."

Hounslow bolted from the office as the rookie cop appeared breathlessly at the doorway to the reception area.

"What, Nick?" Hounslow asked.

Nick swallowed and choked, trying to catch his breath. "Outside ... by the lake ... quick."

Hounslow pushed past him.

✿ ✿ ✿

They sprinted out through the sliding glass doors in the recreation room, across the long stretch of lawn toward the small manmade lake and the woods nearby. There was no doubt that they were all thinking the same thing: *Adam Hounslow has been found floating in the lake!*

But the two other police officers weren't at the lake. They stood thirty yards away at the edge of the woods and flagged their commander. The crowd followed Hounslow and his two men into the woods until they reached another officer who stood somberly by a large tree.

Elizabeth's heart pounded in sympathy as they approached.

"I found this cap," the officer said, holding up a red-and-yellow wool cap with a football team's logo stitched on the front. "Was this your dad's?"

Hounslow nodded quickly. "I got it for him for Christmas. That's his favorite team. Is there anything else?"

The officer pointed wordlessly to the ground. All eyes looked down.

"Oh no," Hounslow whispered.

They were standing by a freshly filled-in hole, about the size of a grave. As they stood staring, the skies opened and it began to rain.

14

Malcolm and Donald caught Manny Hurwitz just as he was locking up the antique shop. The original Miller had sold Miller's Olde Antique Shop to Hurwitz three years before.

"Sorry, guys, I'm closed," Manny said as he turned the key, pulling his jacket up over his head to keep the rain from soaking him. "And I'm late for dinner."

"I'm Malcolm Dubbs and — "

Manny's eyes lit up with recognition and he unlocked the door again, waving them in out of the rain. "Right, right, you guys called. Sorry."

Manny glided through the room, congested with antiques of all kinds. It reminded Malcolm of Donald's office.

"What can I do for you, Mr. Dubbs? Need a few more things for your Village? I'm here to serve," the doughy-faced antiques dealer said, removing his round glasses and polishing them with the edge of his shirt.

"Actually, I need to find out about some items you already sold to us," Malcolm explained.

"I'll help if I can." Manny guided them back to his work area: a large oak desk surrounded by tall bookcases filled with reference books. He squeezed his roly-poly figure past several antiques to get behind the desk to his chair.

Donald pulled a computer printout from his jacket pocket.

"We're trying to trace these three things. Normally we would have a detailed record, but these slipped through the cracks somehow."

Manny read the printout. "Hmm," he grunted and ran his fingers through his thick, wiry hair, then turned to a large ledger next to his desk. He flipped open the long, lined pages and ran his finger up and down the columns.

"You're not on a computerized system," Donald said, as if offended.

"Nope," Manny replied. "Fortunately, I remember these three treasures. They were brought in just a couple of days ago. I won't have to look far."

Malcolm looked at Donald hopefully.

"Yep, there they are. Came in at the same time from the same person. Not valued very highly, I have to confess. But the seller insisted that I broker them to the Historical Village, no matter what the price. I promised I would."

"Who sold them to you?" Malcolm asked.

"According to my register, the owner was Adam Hounslow." Manny looked up from the book. "Any relation to Sheriff Hounslow?"

"Yes," Malcolm answered. "So Adam Hounslow sold the ring, shaving kit, and photo to you — but specifically for my Village."

Manny looked at Donald. "Isn't that what I just said?"

"Did he say anything else? Like, why he was selling them, or why he wanted them in the Village?"

Manny shook his head. "I didn't ask, and he didn't tell. Though I had to wonder why the sheriff's son would sell what were obviously family heirlooms. Is that what this is all about? The sheriff wants them back?"

"No. We're trying to establish — " Donald started to explain, but Malcolm cut him off.

"What did you say? The sheriff's *son*?" Malcolm asked.

"Well, yeah."

"But Adam Hounslow is Sheriff Hounslow's *father.*"

Manny chuckled. "Young-looking father, then. The person who brought that stuff in was — oh, midtwenties."

"You'd better describe him for me," Malcolm said, yanking a pen from his pocket.

Manny handed him a piece of scrap paper from the desk. "That's easy," he said. "He was a good-looking kid. Deep dimples on both sides of his mouth. Smiled a lot. Real friendly. Curly brown hair, nice face, large brown eyes. I kept thinking, *This kid has the looks and charm to be a movie star.*"

15

Because of the rain and the darkness, Sheriff Hounslow brought in large tarps and powered lights. He cleared the area, forcing Jeff, Elizabeth, Mrs. Kottler, and other curious staff members to go back to the recreation room. They crowded around the sliding glass door and watched from a distance. The rookie officer Nick had turned green when he saw the grave-like hole. Hounslow told him to "wait at the center with the rest of the women and children." The sheriff remained, a bleak figure in the pouring rain watching the diggers.

The lights produced an eerie glow in the woods that made the tall, thin trees look like silhouettes of matchsticks.

"It's like a UFO landed out there," Jeff observed.

The officers didn't have to dig for very long before Nick's radio came to life. "We found something … a box. A pretty big box too."

Big enough to hold an old man? Jeff thought. Nobody dared ask that question out loud.

Nick looked green again. "What's in it?" he asked over his radio.

No one answered.

The recreation room door flew open, startling the small crowd. Malcolm walked in and stopped, surprised to have all eyes on him as he lowered his umbrella and took off his jacket. "What happened? Where's Sheriff Hounslow?"

Jeff took Malcolm aside and quietly explained everything.

Just then the radio crackled.

"What?" Nick asked. "What is it?"

"It's ... it's his stuff," the tinny voice of the officer finally reported.

"Stuff?"

"The box is packed with Mr. Hounslow's stuff from his room," the voice on the radio announced. "Looks like there's a second box with ... yeah, more of the same. That's all."

A moment later Sheriff Hounslow burst through the patio doors, clutching his father's baseball cap. "Just what in blazes is going on here?" he shouted to no one in particular.

✿ ✿ ✿

Sheriff Hounslow stared at Malcolm from across the card table in the recreation room. His face was pale, his eyes void of their normal spark. "I hope you have some helpful information."

"Your father's things were sold to the Village through Miller's Antiques — but your father didn't sell them. A young man did."

"Did this young man have a name?" Hounslow asked.

"No," Malcolm replied, "but the store owner, Mr. Hurwitz, remembered him. Good-looking, with deep dimples on both sides of his mouth. Curly brown hair and large brown eyes. Hurwitz said he reminded him of a young Tony Curtis. I guess he looked like a movie star."

Elizabeth and Mrs. Kottler both gasped, then looked at each other.

Hounslow looked up at them warily. "What? What is it?"

"You just described one of my employees," Mrs. Kottler said. "But I'm certain he wouldn't do anything illegal."

"What's his name?"

"Doug Hall."

"Where is he?"

"I believe he went to Hancock after he finished his duties with the residents. He helped bring them back from the Village."

"Why Hancock?" Hounslow asked.

"He often goes there for the weekend," Mrs. Kottler said. "Or sometimes Grantsville. I can't remember."

"Do you have an address or a contact number?"

"I might have one in the office records," she said.

The sheriff looked up at Deputy Peterson, who had just returned from the dig. Peterson nodded.

"Come on, Mrs. Kottler. Let's have a look," he said and accompanied her out the door.

Hounslow flagged one of his other officers. "I want a complete rundown on this Hall kid. Talk to the residents too."

"Mrs. Kottler isn't going to be very pleased with us for bothering the residents again," the officer said.

Hounslow slammed his palm against the tabletop. "I don't care!" he shouted, then wrestled with himself to calm down. "You're right. It won't help our situation if we cause the residents stress. We'll talk to them in the morning. Get everybody out except for the lab boys. I want fingerprints from my father's room and whatever they can get from those boxes in the hole. Secure the areas."

"Yes, sir," the officer said and left.

Hounslow scrubbed a hand over his face and stood up. "Go home. All of you. There's nothing else for you to do here." He waved as if to shoo them away. "Go."

Jeff looked to Malcolm for his assent. Malcolm nodded.

"Come on, Bits," Jeff whispered to Elizabeth, and they left.

Stepping into the hallway, Elizabeth saw something out of the corner of her eye. Down the corridor, something or someone had moved. She didn't say anything to Jeff, but she hesitated in her stride long enough to look quickly. A few doors away, she saw just the outline of the front of someone's legs and shoes peeking out. They silently withdrew into the doorway and disappeared from sight.

Mr. Betterman.

· "What's wrong?" Jeff asked.

"Nothing," she answered and caught up with him down the hall.

Her mind went back to that meeting with Mr. Betterman outside of Adam Hounslow's room. Something was still bothering her ... something her eyes picked up but her brain didn't register. Seeing the legs and shoes down the corridor now put the image within reach, but she still couldn't quite retrieve it.

Halfway home, Jeff finally broke her thoughtful silence. "Okay, tell me. What are you thinking about?"

"Mr. Betterman."

"You can forget about him," Jeff snorted. "Hounslow won't be interested."

"Shoes," she muttered, realizing what had been nagging at her.

"What?"

"His shoes," she said louder, the picture forming in her mind. She had looked at his face, noted the trademark jogging suit and then glanced at his sneakers.

"What about his shoes?" Jeff asked.

Elizabeth turned in the passenger seat to face Jeff. "Dirt and grass were all around the edges of Mr. Betterman's shoes."

16

Elizabeth groggily tugged at the belt on her robe and ambled into the kitchen. Her parents were at the table with half-filled cups of coffee and remnants of grapefruit in front of them.

"Good morning, sleepyhead." Her mom smiled.

"You're going to be late for church," Alan said from behind the Sunday paper.

Elizabeth focused on the front page of the paper, didn't find what she was looking for, then asked, "Is there anything about the nursing home?"

Her dad spread the paper over the top of everything on the table.

"Alan!" her mom protested and quickly retrieved her cup of coffee.

He pointed to a small article on the third page. "There."

Elizabeth moved around the table to look. *Sheriff's Father Missing*, the headline said. The article stated that Adam Hounslow, elderly father of Sheriff Richard Hounslow, had gone missing while attending the opening of the Historical Village. Police were investigating.

"That's all?" she asked.

"Seems so." Alan took the paper. "You made the front page when you disappeared," he added casually.

Elizabeth shivered, and her mom shot a nasty look at her husband.

"Never mind." Elizabeth kissed her father on the top of his silver head as she walked past to get her breakfast. "It's okay, Mom," she said softly.

But the reminder of her own disappearance — and the reason for it — stayed with her through her breakfast, her quick shower, and the scramble to get to church.

To her parents' annoyance, they were a few minutes late and had to squeeze into the back row during the first hymn. In front of them, Jeff turned around to smile at her. Elizabeth wiggled her fingers at him and smiled back.

The service proceeded as usual until, right before his sermon, Reverend Armstrong suggested that the congregation pray for Adam Hounslow and the sheriff. "We've had our share of close calls and disappearances in this community," he said. "The anxiety this is causing our sheriff must be great. We should remember him in our hearts and our prayers until his father is returned safe and sound." He led the church in a brief but eloquent prayer on behalf of the Hounslows.

Elizabeth wondered if the church had prayed for her when she disappeared. Maybe that helped to bring her back from the other time. *Maybe it'll help bring Adam Hounslow back from wherever he is.*

On the way out of church after the service, Elizabeth saw small clusters of her friends chatting amiably in the hall and on the steps — Jeff was with them. She waved but didn't join them. Instead, she walked toward the small grove of trees along the east side of the church.

Adam Hounslow's disappearance hadn't affected the beauty of this Sunday morning. Shafts of sunlight shot through the long branches, and everything seemed bright and clean after the rain. Elizabeth stepped into the light, hoping it might burn away the darkness hanging on the edge of her memories. Somehow whatever had happened to Adam Hounslow was linked to what had happened to her. She knew it. She didn't know how or why, but she sensed it. The thought of her nightmare — the bath, the polluted water, the switch in time — and the image of Mr. Betterman sitting in her dark bedroom saying, "I know who you are . . . *Sarah*."

"Excuse me."

Elizabeth jumped and spun around.

Elizabeth had never seen the young woman before. "Sorry. I didn't mean to startle you. You're Elizabeth Forde, right?"

"Yes," Elizabeth said warily.

"I'm Jennifer Reeves. I was thinking about Adam Hounslow's disappearance, and I remembered that you were missing for a while too, weren't you?" She squinted as the shaft of light shifted and bleached her face.

Elizabeth was perplexed. "Who are you?"

"You disappeared under some very mysterious circumstances. I was wondering what you thought about Adam Hounslow's disappearance," the woman continued.

Elizabeth frowned. "Why are you asking me about this?"

"I just want to talk to you, that's all."

"You're a reporter, aren't you?"

"Well, actually — "

"Please, leave me alone," Elizabeth said.

"Look, it'll help a lot of people if you'll just — "

"Get away from me!" Elizabeth shouted. It was enough to draw the attention of those still mingling outside the church. Jeff broke away from the small group he'd been talking to and raced toward her.

"What's wrong?"

Jennifer Reeves turned and walked off, as if the whole scene had nothing to do with her.

"She's a reporter," Elizabeth whispered.

Malcolm strode quickly across the lawn toward Elizabeth,

followed by Elizabeth's parents, Alan and Jane Forde. Elizabeth felt foolish for the fuss she'd made. "There's no problem. I'm sorry."

Jeff wouldn't let her get away with it. "That woman was a reporter," he announced.

"A reporter!" Malcolm exclaimed.

"I'll have a word or two with Jerry Anderson," Elizabeth's dad growled. Jerry was the editor of Fawlt Line's only daily newspaper.

"I don't think she works for him," Malcolm said as he watched the woman climb into a small rental car and drive off.

Jeff put his arm around Elizabeth. "Are you all right?" he asked anxiously.

She nodded. "Yeah. It's no big deal. She just annoyed me."

The five of them headed back toward the church and the parking lot beyond. Sheriff Hounslow was waiting for them next to his squad car.

"Good morning, Sheriff," Malcolm said.

"Any chance of talking to all of you?" Hounslow asked.

Malcolm glanced around at the others. "Why don't we go back to my cottage? Mrs. Packer makes a wonderful Sunday brunch."

○ ○ ○

Amidst the clinks and rattles of the cups and dishes on Malcolm's dining room table, the small group chitchatted about the weather, the Village, and anything other than the subject they were supposed to discuss. Alan Forde launched into a lengthy discussion about the air currents that were contributing to the weather patterns they were experiencing. His wife quietly asked him to *shush*. Finally, Mrs. Packer was complimented by all for a delicious lunch, and all eyes drifted to Sheriff Hounslow. He had called this meeting, so he needed to start it.

The sheriff wiped his mouth with a napkin and tossed it onto the table. "We haven't found Doug Hall yet," he announced. "We're still running a check on him."

"What happens next?" Alan asked.

"I don't know." Hounslow shook his head as he pushed away from the table. "What I have to say, I don't say easily. You know I'm not a big fan of all that time travel nonsense. But I didn't sleep a wink last night because I couldn't get it off my mind. I still think it's crazy, but I want to hear about it anyway. My father's missing and — " He suddenly stopped, unable to go on. He turned away from them until he could compose himself.

"Your father's missing and, like any good detective, you want to consider all the possibilities," Malcolm said, giving him time to recover.

The sheriff cleared his throat. "Something like that. I know you believe that Fawlt Line is sitting on top of some kind of a *time* fault. You say that's why Elizabeth disappeared and how that clown who called himself King Arthur slipped through. So now I'm wondering . . . I mean . . ."

"You're wondering if it's possible that your father stumbled onto another fault — a doorway, if you will — while he was in the mining row houses," Malcolm said.

The sheriff nodded. "But you have to help me with this 'stumbling' part. You make it sound like he tripped on a rock and suddenly fell into some other time. Is that possible — like an accident?"

"Maybe." Malcolm gave his ear a tug. "Though I'm not a big believer in accidents or coincidences. I'm inclined toward a more providential point of view."

"Providential or not, I don't think this is an accident either," Hounslow said. "Whatever happened to my father happened on purpose."

"What makes you so sure?" Jeff asked.

The question was harmless enough, but it touched a deep place in the sheriff. He struggled for a moment, then finally said,

"My father and I haven't been getting along lately. I practically had to carry him out of the house he'd lived in for years. It was too big for him to take care of. And my dad was showing the early signs of Alzheimer's disease."

"I'm sorry. That's very difficult," Alan said softly.

"He had reached a point of despair in his life like I'd never seen before — not even when my mother died." Hounslow gestured to Elizabeth. "You saw how grouchy he was at the center. Well, that wasn't my dad. He was always a good-humored man. But twice in the last several months — when he was still living in his house — I went to see him and actually thought he was dead. He was just lying there with virtually no vital signs. I called the ambulance and everything."

"What was wrong with him?" Elizabeth asked.

"The doctors didn't have an explanation, except that it might've been psychological. They thought he was overwhelmed with the desire to die." The sheriff fiddled with the tablecloth. "Going to the retirement center was probably the icing on the cake. That's what I mean when I say it wasn't an accident. I think my father ran away somehow or, more likely went off somewhere to kill himself."

The room went stiff with silence. Hounslow swallowed hard, and Jeff and Elizabeth looked at each other uneasily. They weren't sure how to react to this man who traditionally annoyed them. Beyond his bark and bluster, he was suddenly very human. Alan and Jane stared at the table. Elizabeth suspected that they were remembering their own feelings when she had disappeared.

Malcolm looked deeply moved, but folded his arms and stood quietly for a moment. Finally, he said, "Do you really believe that?"

"Oh, yes," Hounslow replied. "I've thought and thought about my father's behavior yesterday. There was a certain peace, a strange calm, as if he knew this was going to happen. He *knew*."

The sheriff lowered his head and said nothing else. Malcolm looked at Jeff, Elizabeth, Alan, and Jane as if to say that now was the right time for them to leave. They nodded, then quietly stood up and walked out of the dining room.

"You'll bring Elizabeth home?" Alan asked Jeff.

"Yes, sir."

"Keep the reporters away from her," Jane admonished him.

"Yes, ma'am."

They made their way to the front door and their car beyond. Elizabeth and Jeff slipped through Malcolm's den, then outside through the large glass doors and sat on a bench on the patio.

"I should tell him about the dirt and grass on the edges of Mr. Betterman's shoes," Elizabeth said. She stretched like a cat in the hot sun.

"He wouldn't believe you," Jeff said.

Elizabeth looked doubtful. "I think he would. He looks ready to believe anything that'll help him find his dad."

Jeff frowned. "Even if he did get emotional, he's still the same stubborn man. Do you think he'll believe that a man in a wheelchair suddenly leapt up to kidnap his father?"

"But we don't know that Mr. Betterman really needs to be in a wheelchair. What if he's been faking it all along?"

Jeff thought about it for a moment. "Mrs. Kottler might know. Or the records at the retirement center would probably say why he's in the chair."

"Probably."

They looked at each other, then Jeff smiled. "What do you say we take a little Sunday drive over to the retirement center and find out for ourselves?"

❀ ❀ ❀

In the dining room, Hounslow stood up. "It's more than I can believe."

Malcolm smiled. "It's more than any of us could believe. If it hadn't happened to Elizabeth — if she hadn't experienced that other time firsthand — I'd be skeptical too. But she did experience it. So did Jeff. We saw their time twins for ourselves."

"Your so-called King Arthur didn't have a time twin," Hounslow argued.

"That was different," Malcolm said. "And I can't explain why any more than I can explain how your father might have disappeared in the row house. But he might have. By accident or on purpose. Only he knows right now."

"And you really think he's alive?"

For the first time since their conversation began, Malcolm looked troubled. "I wish I could say so for sure, but I can't."

Hounslow nodded sadly. "Well, I have to go back to the department. We've got an All Points Bulletin out on Doug Hall. Right now he's the only solid lead we have."

"Mind if I tag along?"

17

The retirement center was thick with the lethargy of the Sunday heat. At least, that's what Jeff and Elizabeth tried to tell themselves. As they searched for Mrs. Kottler, they couldn't seem to get more than a quick "hello" from the residents they saw in the halls or sitting in the recreation room.

"Are they always so pleasant?" Jeff whispered sarcastically.

"Something's wrong," Elizabeth whispered back. "Maybe they're still upset about the death of Mrs. Schultz and the disappearance of Mr. Hounslow."

"Maybe."

They found Dolly Higgins sitting alone in her room. She looked up apprehensively when Elizabeth knocked on her door and entered.

"Hi, Dolly!" Elizabeth said cheerfully.

"What are you doing here, child? It's Sunday."

"I'm allowed to come visit you if I want to, aren't I?" Elizabeth smiled.

Dolly frowned. "If you want, I suppose. But . . . I'm feeling tired. I really shouldn't have visitors right now."

"Well, it's a perfect afternoon for a nap," Elizabeth replied sympathetically and scooted Jeff out of the room.

"This is weird," she said when they were out of earshot. "And Mrs. Kottler isn't anywhere around. Let's go look for the files."

Elizabeth led Jeff through the front reception area to Mrs. Kottler's office. Her door was locked, and Elizabeth felt relieved. Sneaking around in the filing cabinets suddenly struck her as a bad idea.

"What about this one?" Jeff asked, moving to a door on the opposite wall.

Elizabeth didn't remember where it led. "It might be a closet."

Jeff jiggled the handle, and the door opened easily. He peeked in. "It looks like a little kitchen." He disappeared into the room, so that Elizabeth could only hear his voice. "Hey, there's another door."

Elizabeth glanced around to make sure no one could see them, then followed him in. "I don't think we should do this," she said.

But Jeff had gone through a door at the other end of the kitchen area — into Mrs. Kottler's office. He was already at one of the filing cabinets, rifling through the manila folders. "Betterman ... Betterman ..." he muttered.

"I don't like this, Jeff," Elizabeth said. "It's got to be against the law."

"We're not stealing anything. A quick peek at Betterman's file is all we want."

"Well hurry," she said. She heard something in the other room and tiptoed through the kitchen. She peered out the door into the reception area. Still empty. Then unmistakable sounds from down the hall sent a hard chill through her body. It was the whirring of an electric motor, and Mrs. Kottler's voice saying, "Now, Mr. Betterman, I know what you're thinking ..."

Elizabeth gently closed the door and raced back into Mrs. Kottler's office. "Jeff!" she whispered.

"Found it!" he said.

"Put it away! They're coming!" she cried.

Jeff looked stricken and fumbled as he tried to shove the file back into the drawer.

The whir and the voice were closer, probably in the reception area. Jeff dropped the file. It fell to the floor and sent pages exploding into several directions.

Elizabeth's mind seized up. All she could think to do was create a diversion somehow by running through the little kitchen and into the reception area. Then Mrs. Kottler's key turned in the lock.

It must've been quite a picture for Mrs. Kottler and Mr. Betterman when they entered the room. Elizabeth stood at the kitchen door with her hand clasped over her mouth. Jeff crouched over the scattered pages.

"Good heavens!" Mrs. Kottler cried.

"What's going on here?" Betterman growled.

Jeff stood up, but didn't speak. Mr. Betterman drove his wheelchair forward and snatched up a page from the floor.

"Elizabeth!" Mrs. Kottler exclaimed when she noticed her near the kitchen. "What's the meaning of this?"

"This is *my* file," Mr. Betterman said. "What are you up to? Why are you looking at my file?"

Jeff blurted out the truth, "Because we think you had something to do with Adam Hounslow's disappearance."

"What?" Mrs. Kottler shrieked.

Elizabeth moved to Jeff's side. "Mrs. Kottler, there's a lot going on here that you don't — "

"Do you know I could have you arrested for this? How dare you break into my office and steal one of my resident's files?"

Mr. Betterman waved at Mrs. Kottler to be quiet. "What are you talking about? What makes you think I had anything to do with whatever happened to Adam Hounslow?"

"The dirt and grass on your shoes after Mr. Hounslow disappeared, for one thing," Elizabeth said. "I saw it when you stopped me from going into his room. Your shoes were filthy, like you'd been out in the woods where they found Mr. Hounslow's stuff."

Mr. Betterman clucked his tongue and shook his head at her.

"Girl, you have too much time on your hands. I'll tell you what happened — "

"No, Mr. Betterman," Mrs. Kottler said coldly. "Don't satisfy their warped curiosity."

Betterman went on anyway. "I hit a pothole in the lawn, and it sent me and my wheelchair tumbling. My feet skidded along the dirt and grass. It was very painful for me."

Jeff and Elizabeth were both at a loss for words, but Jeff wasn't ready to give up. "So why do you keep calling Elizabeth *Sarah*, huh? Why are you trying to scare her?"

"This is ridiculous," Mr. Betterman snarled and abruptly spun his wheelchair around to leave. "I leave them in your charge, Mrs. Kottler."

Mrs. Kottler glared at them. "I don't care if you are related to Malcolm Dubbs or the Prince of Wales. I want you both out of here ... now."

"Mrs. Kottler, listen," Elizabeth said quickly. "You don't know what's going on. Something's happening here and Mr. Betterman's in the middle of it."

"I'm so disappointed in you, Elizabeth," Mrs. Kottler said. Then, drawing herself up, she took a deep breath and said, "Your volunteer services are no longer wanted here. I should call the police, but I won't *this time*. Now go."

"Mrs. Schultz's death ... Adam Hounslow's disappearance ... *please*, Mrs. Kottler! Check into Mr. Betterman. That's the only reason we did this. We wanted to see if he really should be in a wheelchair."

Mrs. Kottler pointed to the door. "Go."

Jeff moved past her and pulled at Elizabeth's arm. "Let's go. It's no use."

Elizabeth took a few steps, then suddenly turned on Mrs. Kottler. "You're in on it too, aren't you?"

Mrs. Kottler gasped indignantly.

"You're part of it somehow. That's the only way it could go on. You're working with Mr. Betterman."

"Get out now, or I'll have the police arrest you for trespassing!" the director shouted.

Elizabeth scowled, but turned away silently. Whatever was going on with Mr. Betterman, the retirement center, and Adam Hounslow wouldn't be uncovered by her — not like this. But she knew as she walked out of the office that she wouldn't be free of her nightmares until the truth was known.

18

Deputy Bob Peterson dropped another collection of faxes onto the table in the police station's conference room. "A few more answers from the nursing homes," he announced.

Hounslow looked up. "Anything from Hancock? Grantsville?"

"No," Peterson said. "Doug Hall seems to have dropped off the face of the earth."

"Maybe *he* slipped through your time fault," Hounslow jabbed at Malcolm, who was flipping through faxes at the end of the table.

"Jeff and Elizabeth saw him pushing Betterman's wheelchair out of the Village, remember?" Malcolm countered.

"Which is the only reason I'm still hoping that my dad is with Hall somewhere."

Malcolm leaned back in his chair. He hadn't thought of that possibility. "What did Betterman say when you asked him about Doug Hall? Obviously he was one of the last to see him."

" 'He's a nice boy' was about all Betterman had to offer. He said Doug dropped him off at the center and then took off for a 'wild weekend away,' " the sheriff grumbled. "What kind of wild weekend can anyone have in Hancock or Grantsville?"

"What did the rest of the residents say about him?"

"The women at the center loved him. Apparently he was a real charmer."

Malcolm sighed and gestured to the papers. "Why would such a charming young man switch jobs so often? And all in nursing homes. Sometimes more than every six months in the past six years."

"Sheriff," Peterson interrupted, "I checked on missing persons reports in all the towns where Doug Hall worked before now."

Hounslow grunted appreciatively. "Good thinking, Bob."

"I don't know what to make of it, but" — he held up a couple of the pages — "it looks like there have been a couple of cases of people disappearing from areas where Doug Hall worked."

"*What?*" Hounslow roared.

○ ○ ○

Jeff drove Elizabeth home. A brooding silence settled over them in the car. They felt frustrated and helpless. To know that something bad — perhaps even *evil*, as Frieda Schultz had said — was going on and not be able to do anything about it was more than either of them could stand. Elizabeth was surprised to realize that she'd moved from being afraid of Mr. Betterman to being angry at him.

Her parents were in the middle of their usual Sunday afternoon activities when she and Jeff arrived. Her father was pulling weeds in the garden, while her mother folded clothes in the laundry room.

"I'm going to get out of my church clothes and into some jeans," Elizabeth told Jeff.

"Wait a minute," her mom called out. "Take these clothes up with you."

Elizabeth walked into the laundry room to grab her shirts and pants from the rack. "Thanks, Mom." She noticed that her uniform from the retirement center was included in the collection. "Oh, I forgot about this," she said.

"It was filthy," Mrs. Forde declared. "And you left some things in the pockets. I almost washed them."

"Sorry," Elizabeth said and retrieved a couple of tissues and a scrap of paper. "Thanks for cleaning it."

"Well, you can't go to the center tomorrow with a dirty uniform."

Elizabeth looked at Jeff, then back at her mother. "I'm not going back to the center, Mom."

"You're not?"

Elizabeth sighed. "You tell her while I change," she said to Jeff.

"Thanks a lot," he answered.

Elizabeth took her clothes up to her room, hung them in her closet, and quickly changed into a T-shirt and jeans. She was tying the shoelaces on her sneakers when her eye caught the scrap of paper her mother had pulled from her uniform pocket.

"Gloxinia" an elderly scrawl stated simply at the top. Elizabeth felt a tug at her heart. It was Frieda Schultz's handwriting. She'd written down the name of her flowers for Elizabeth the very day she'd died. Elizabeth gently took the scrap and unfolded it. *Poor Frieda*, she thought. *Will anyone ever know what really happened to you? Why did you cry so mournfully?*

Then Elizabeth's eyes widened. Beneath the name of the flowers, Mrs. Schultz had scribbled, "*Help. Fawlt Line Cinema. 10:00 p.m. 22nd.*"

She stared at the piece of paper for a moment, trying to make it register. Why had Mrs. Schultz written such a cryptic message?

Because she was scared, Elizabeth realized. She was trying to communicate with Elizabeth while she had the chance. But what did it mean?

Shoving the scrap into her pocket, she made her way downstairs and found Jeff in the den with her mom. Her dad had joined them, grimy and sweaty from the garden. When she walked in, her parents looked at her with worried expressions.

"You never should have gone into that office," Alan Forde reprimanded her. "It's against the law and, if your suspicions are true, potentially dangerous."

Elizabeth hung her head. "I know. But we never could've gotten the police in there. It seemed like a good idea at the time."

"You're both lucky Mrs. Kottler didn't have you locked up," Mrs. Forde said.

Jeff fidgeted in his chair. "I wish she had called the police. Chances are it would've forced them to check into what we've been saying."

Mr. Forde chuckled. "All you have are suspicions, guesses, and feelings. The police have no way of forcing Betterman to admit to anything. And it's entirely possible that you're wrong."

"What?" Elizabeth asked, stunned.

"If you want to play detective, then play it well," Alan said. "A good detective considers all possibilities, I heard Malcolm say today."

Elizabeth pulled the scrap from her pocket. "If I'm wrong, then what about this?" She passed the note around. "It's a message from Frieda Schultz — right before she died. She said she was writing down the name of her flowers. I forgot all about it till Mom found it today."

Her dad pondered the note for a moment. "Maybe she wrote the name of the flowers over top a note she'd written to herself."

Elizabeth glared at him. "Oh, Daddy, you're as bad as Sheriff Hounslow! Why would she write 'help' on a note to herself?"

"Maybe the cinema needs it," he offered.

Mrs. Forde rubbed her chin. "But Fawlt Line doesn't have a cinema anymore."

"It doesn't?" Alan asked.

"It closed down a few years ago, remember?" she replied.

"Malcolm moved it to the Village," Jeff said.

"Yes, yes!" Mr. Forde interjected, the light coming on in his eyes. "He said it was a perfect example of a 1930s movie theater, with its balconies and gold trimmings and the big, old burgundy curtain."

"I think we should take the note to the sheriff's department," Jeff suggested.

"Sensible thinking, Jeff," Mr. Forde commended him.

In the Volkswagen on the way, Jeff glanced knowingly over at Elizabeth. "You know what today is, right?" he asked.

"Sunday?"

"The twenty-second. Mrs. Schultz's note said ten o'clock tonight."

O O O

The sheriff department was a beehive of activity. Jeff and Elizabeth made their way past the harried-looking men and women who were shouting into phones and darting back and forth between the small offices. The center of the activity was a conference room at the end of the hall, where Hounslow was barking orders at whoever happened to be handy.

"I don't care if it's late on a Sunday afternoon or midnight on Christmas Eve! Tell them this is an emergency!" The sheriff shouted at one frazzled woman, who retreated like a kicked puppy.

Jeff and Elizabeth walked in quietly, spotted Malcolm, and joined him at his end of the table.

"What's going on, Malcolm?"

"They're calling police departments around the country," he explained. "We found a connection between Doug Hall's employment and other unsolved missing persons cases."

Elizabeth gasped. "You think Doug *kidnapped* Adam Hounslow?"

"We don't know anything at this point. Because it's Sunday,

we've had a hard time tracking down the investigating officers, or even someone who might be able to pull a file. All we need are some details about the missing people." Malcolm rubbed his face wearily. "I'm afraid this could take all night. There must be a way to talk to at least one of the investigators face-to-face."

"Look at this!" Hounslow shouted to no one in particular. He was pointing at the accumulated bits of information in front of him on the table. "Why didn't we see this? If it were a snake it would've bit me." He turned to Malcolm. "Look, in most of these cases, maybe all of them, the missing person disappeared in — well, here. Look for yourself!"

Malcolm flipped through some pages. "This one disappeared in a historic bed-and-breakfast in Boston — "

"Three blocks from the nursing home where Hall worked," Hounslow added.

"This one disappeared in a Baltimore museum," Malcolm continued. "A historic mansion, another museum, a library, the oldest building in a college, and ... a restaurant?"

"It was closed," Hounslow explained.

"So they all disappeared in historical places," Jeff said.

"Coincidence?" Deputy Peterson asked.

"What do *you* think?" Hounslow challenged him. "You've got Doug Hall and others disappearing in places of historical interest. Just like my dad. How did the investigating officers miss this? Why wasn't Hall ever arrested?"

"Who would've made a connection before now?" Malcolm asked, in defense of all the investigators who weren't there to answer for themselves.

Hounslow waved his arms at his staff like a mad conductor. "Don't just stand around! Get back on the phones! I want this confirmed! I want to know about the rest of these cases!"

Everyone scattered except Malcolm, Jeff, and Elizabeth. Hounslow slumped into his chair and put his face in his hands.

There was a pause long enough to give Elizabeth the courage to step forward, the scrap of paper from Mrs. Schultz in her outstretched hand. "Sheriff? We thought you might want to see this."

He lifted his head up slightly and took the scrap. "What is it?"

"Mrs. Schultz wrote it before she died." Elizabeth rounded the table and guided him through the message. "Gloxinia is the name of the flower she had on her nightstand — the plant Mr. Betterman took away."

"Oh, please. You're not going to start on this whole Betterman business again," Hounslow complained.

"No, sir," Elizabeth continued. "But look at the rest of the note … 'Help!' Then, 'the cinema at ten o'clock' tonight."

"Meaning?"

"Meaning that maybe something will happen there tonight," she said, puzzled that he hadn't figured it out for himself.

Hounslow groaned then tossed the note onto the table. "All right. If I have someone available, I'll try to remember to send him over."

"The cinema's at the Village," Malcolm said. "I can have one of my security guards check on it."

"Whatever," Hounslow said dismissively, spreading his arms over the pages and pages of reports. "This is going to take too long. And probably none of it has anything to do with my father's disappearance." He suddenly pounded the tabletop. "Blast it, Hall! Where are you?"

Malcolm leaned forward and thoughtfully picked up a small, clipped stack of papers. He looked at them for a moment before turning to Hounslow. "Sheriff, this case happened only a year ago in Annapolis. Doug Hall worked at a nursing home on West Street, and a man disappeared in the Colonial Book Shop nearby. If I flew down in my plane, I'd be there within an hour."

"I can't ask you to do that," Hounslow said.

"You don't have to; I'm suggesting it myself. I could talk to one of the detectives — hopefully the one who handled the case — providing you can use your authority with a supervisor. It's worth a try, right?"

Hounslow looked as if he might argue but changed his mind. "All right, if you don't have anything better to do." Which was Hounslow's way of saying he was grateful.

"Do you want to come with me, Jeff? It'd be helpful to have a partner."

"Are you kidding? You couldn't keep me away!"

Elizabeth cleared her throat loudly.

"I'm sorry, Elizabeth," Malcolm said. "I think three will make things a little complicated and crowded. We don't want to look like we're ganging up on the poor detective."

"That's okay," she replied, gesturing for Jeff to come talk to her privately. They retreated to a corner.

"What's wrong?" Jeff whispered.

"What about the cinema at ten o'clock?"

"Malcolm will have one of his guards check it out."

"And what am I supposed to do in the meantime?" Elizabeth was annoyed.

"We won't be gone that long. We'll be home in no time at all."

"Mind if I wait for you at Malcolm's?" Elizabeth asked as a concession. "I don't want to be far away if you come back with any news."

"Suits me," Jeff said.

Jeff drove Elizabeth to the cottage, and Malcolm arrived a minute later in his Jeep. Mrs. Packer had been watching for them and ran out to the driveway to greet them.

"What's wrong?" Malcolm called, without getting out of the car.

"Donald Nelson keeps calling for you. He says he needs to talk to you right away."

"Probably some business to do with the Village," Malcolm mumbled to himself. To Mrs. Packer he said: "Tell him I'll call him on my cell while I drive to the airport, otherwise I'll be back later tonight, probably around nine-thirty."

Mrs. Packer frowned. "He was insistent — to the point of being rude."

"I'm sure you handled him with your usual tact," Malcolm said. "Oh — and will you call the security office and ask them to check out the Old Cinema at ten o'clock? Tell them it's important."

"Yes, sir," she said. "At ten o'clock?"

Malcolm nodded as he put his window up. "Let's go, Jeff," he called out.

Jeff had already gotten into the passenger seat and was talking to Elizabeth through the passenger window. He kissed her lightly and gently stroked her hair. "We'll be back in no time at all."

She nodded and stepped away from the car.

Malcolm reversed out of the driveway, and Mrs. Packer and Elizabeth stood side by side waving as the Jeep pulled away.

19

Annapolis Detective Steve White had been contacted by Sheriff Hounslow just as he returned from his traditional Sunday afternoon spent crabbing on the river. Even though he'd showered and changed clothes, he still smelled of bay water and fish. His face was beet red and looked like a dome light sitting atop his broad shoulders and short, stocky body.

He shook Malcolm's and Jeff's hands. "I don't think I put enough suntan lotion on," he explained, gesturing for Malcolm and Jeff to sit down in the wooden visitors chairs opposite his desk.

"Thank you for seeing us on your day off," Malcolm said. "We appreciate your help."

Detective White tilted his head slightly. "Pretty odd circumstances, I'd say. Particularly your sheriff sending two civilians to look at our files. If he hadn't called my commander first, you'd have wasted your trip." He slid two manila folders across the desk toward Malcolm. "These are copies of what we have. You can take them back to Hounslow. Did I understand that his father disappeared?"

Malcolm nodded and picked up the file. "Right. It's quite a mystery."

"Then let's compare some notes," White suggested. "I was the detective on the two cases of missing persons we had here at the time. The first was Ralph McInery. He was living at the Arundel Nursing Home where Doug Hall worked. McInery's the one who went into the Colonial Book Shop on West Street and, as far as anyone knows, never came out again."

"How was that possible? Somebody must have noticed."

"It happened at the height of the tourist season last summer. People were in and out of the shop constantly. The employees simply didn't remember what happened after he came in. The whole business was reported by Jack Greene, a friend of McInery's from the home. They were shopping together. Greene said McInery went into the store but didn't come out again."

"Back door?"

"Yes, but the manager of the store was there the whole time doing inventory. Nobody came through." White pointed to the second file. "That case involved a guy named Thomas Finney. He also lived at the Arundel Nursing Home and disappeared from an antique shop in one of those old houses near the bay. It was during the tourist season too, toward the end of the summer. He went in with a group of senior citizens but didn't come out again. We nearly tore the house apart looking for him."

"I guess the big question is: Why wasn't Doug Hall brought in for questioning?" Malcolm asked.

White grimaced. "On what basis? It's not as if we had any evidence of foul play. All we could do was establish that Hall knew the missing people and was in the area when they disappeared."

"What do you mean, 'in the area'?"

"He was in the Colonial Book Shop the day McInery disappeared — ditto the antique shop when Finney went bye-bye. But that wasn't unusual. Hall was responsible for transporting the residents when they went shopping. I couldn't arrest him for doing his job."

"Of course not," Malcolm said as he thumbed through the file.

"Don't get me wrong," White went on. "I suspected Hall when I realized he'd been an employee in other towns where old folks disappeared. And, frankly, I didn't like him. He was too slick, if you know what I mean. So we kept an eye on him. But it didn't lead anywhere, and when Hall decided to leave town we had no grounds to stop him."

"Did you ever find the missing people?" Jeff asked.

"Nope. Both cases are unsolved. Without a kidnapper's note or discovery of a body, the feeling was that the two men had run away of their own free will."

Malcolm raised an eyebrow. "Why did you think that?"

"Because of their states of mind before they disappeared. We talked to folks they knew at the home and learned that both men were extremely unhappy there. But before they disappeared they seemed to have a certain peace of mind — like suicides sometimes have before they do the deed."

"Hmm," said Malcolm. "That's how Sheriff Hounslow described his father before he disappeared."

"That's interesting. Does he think his father committed suicide?"

Malcolm shrugged. "I don't think he's ruling out anything at this point."

"It's gotta be awful for him — investigating his own father's disappearance. He said it happened at that historical village? I saw something about it in the newspapers. Maybe I'll make a weekend of it and come up with my family sometime."

"Please do," Malcolm said. "Give me enough warning and I'll make sure you get in free."

"Thanks." The detective looked genuinely pleased.

"Did any of your investigators make the connection that the two missing men both disappeared in places of historical interest?"

"Not really. Hey, all of the buildings in this part of town are historical. We would've written it off as coincidence. But there was one small curious bit of information that came up. I didn't think much of it at the time. Even if I had, I'm not sure I would've figured out what it meant. Hold on a sec."

Malcolm and Jeff waited while White searched through the files.

"Here," he finally said. "The missing men had previously done business with the places where they disappeared."

Malcolm sat up. "What?"

White seemed pleased to get Malcolm's attention so dramatically. "McInery had sold his entire library — a lot of books, I guess — to the Colonial Book Shop two weeks before he disappeared. And Finney sold several boxes of family heirlooms to the antique shop. Does that mean something to you?"

"Adam Hounslow sold some of his belongings to my Village. But he did it through Doug Hall and a local antique shop!"

A question suddenly occurred to Jeff. "How did the people at the nursing home respond when McInery and Finney disappeared?"

White rubbed his chin for a moment, speaking slowly as he tried to remember. "If I remember correctly, they were agitated and alarmed. Pretty much as you'd expect people to be after their friends go missing. Some were very suspicious, I think. And, you know, now that you mention it, they seemed to close up on me. Nobody wanted to talk or answer questions. As if they were scared. But I figured that was normal, all things considered. Why?"

"Because that's how everybody was acting at the Fawlt Line Retirement Center today," Jeff replied. Malcolm looked at Jeff with interest.

"Pretty normal, I'd guess," White concluded. "Those nursing homes can be tightly wound communities. The people who live there sometimes circle the wagons to ward off any outside threat." He paused, put his hands on his desk, and stood up.

"Well, look, if you two will excuse me, I have a family at home who need me to get the meat out of the crabs I caught today."

Malcolm and Jeff walked outside with Detective White and Malcolm thanked him again for taking the time to talk to them.

White shook their hands again. "Don't hesitate to call me tomorrow if you need any more information. I hope Sheriff Hounslow finds his father."

Malcolm and Jeff got into their rental car and drove back to the small airfield on the outskirts of town.

"Too many coincidences," Jeff said.

Malcolm agreed. "These aren't coincidences. They're patterns of some kind. But what do they mean? What in the world is Hall up to?"

20

The summer light had moved across the wall and was fading into night when Sheriff Hounslow poured himself his seventh cup of coffee. He set it on the littered table and stretched with a loud groan. The thought of yet another round with the reports didn't appeal to him at all. He wanted to get out and *do* something to find his father. But there wasn't much to do unless Doug Hall presented him with a ransom note of some sort — *if* Doug Hall was the guilty party. Hounslow could only go through the reports and hope to find a link, a piece of information, *anything* that might give him a lead to his father's whereabouts. He sat down and wearily picked up the cup to take a sip of the bitter liquid.

"Sheriff!" Deputy Peterson shouted, causing Hounslow to dribble hot coffee down his chin.

"Doggone it, Bob!" Hounslow exclaimed as he grabbed a napkin and tried to keep the coffee off his shirt.

"Oh, sorry," Peterson stammered. "I just thought you'd want to know that Doug Hall's car was seen at a boarding house out-side of Grantsville."

"Did you get the address?"

"Yeah."

That was all the sheriff needed to hear. "Let's go!" he barked, grabbing his hat and heading for the door.

"But that's outside our jurisdiction! The Grantsville Police will — "

Hounslow brushed past him. "I'm sure the Grantsville Police will appreciate our help. I'm going."

Deputy Peterson helplessly chased his boss down the hall.

○ ○ ○

Elizabeth and Mrs. Packer were in Malcolm's study playing checkers when the phone on the desk rang. The housekeeper reached over to get it.

"Dubbs' Cottage ... Where are you, Mr. Dubbs?"

At the mention of Malcolm's name, Elizabeth perked up. "Are they back? Did they find out anything?"

Mrs. Packer signaled her to be quiet. "Oh, that's too bad."

"What?" Elizabeth asked.

"They're going to be late," Mrs. Packer told her, covering the mouthpiece. "They're grounded in Annapolis due to cloud cover." She turned her attention back to Malcolm. "Elizabeth is chomping at the bit to know what you learned ,.. Yes. Oh, and Don Nelson has been calling for you. I thought you were going to call him ... Oh, I see. Do you have his number? ... Yes. Thank you. We'll be here."

"Well?" Elizabeth asked anxiously.

"He said they've learned plenty, and he'll tell you all about it in a few hours — if your parents will let you stay here and wait."

Elizabeth looked at her apprehensively. "Do you mind?"

"Not at all."

"Then I'll call them."

○ ○ ○

"Sorry it took so long to get back to you, Donald," Malcolm apologized over a crackly cell phone line. "My cell phone battery went dead and I didn't have the charger in the car."

"Quite all right." Donald Nelson cradled the phone between

his cheek and shoulder as he tugged at a list he'd placed on the edge of his desk.

"What's so important?"

Donald cleared his throat. "Well, because of the situation with Adam Hounslow's belongings, I thought I'd double-check any other local purchases we've made for the Village."

"Smart thinking."

"I've been going through the inventory records, cross-referencing what we've purchased from all the local antique shops, and discovered a rather bizarre connection."

The line hissed for a moment. "We're full of bizarre connections tonight," Malcolm said. "What did you find?"

"As you know," Donald began, "the antiques we bought for the Village were from a wide variety of sources. A hurricane lamp from the Andrews family, a turn-of-the-century sewing machine from the Smiths, china from the Stevensons. Unless we hit on a family auction or bankruptcy, our antique purchases are generally quite diversified."

"We get a lot of different things from a lot of different places," Malcolm said simply. "You're right, I'm well aware of that. Is there more?"

"Yes, sir. As I've been tracing our local purchases, I've discovered that the majority of the antiques locally were supplied by a minority of families, fewer than a dozen in all."

"In other words," said Malcolm, "we got a lot of different things from only a few places. I'm with you so far. Is that it?"

"No, sir," Donald replied. "I contacted the antique shops — no small feat on a Sunday, by the way — and they led me to the names of the people who sold the antiques to them in the first place. I then began calling those names to talk to whoever made the sale. I didn't get through to them all, but those I actually contacted had no idea what I was talking about."

"What do you mean?"

"They were families who had no idea that their heirlooms had been donated or sold. When I asked who had the authority to sell the items, in almost every case it was, say, an elderly mother or father."

"Like Adam Hounslow, for example."

"Naturally, I asked the families how I might get in touch with their elderly parents, and they all said I could visit them at the nursing home where they lived." Donald paused. "Three guesses which nursing home."

The line hissed and sputtered again. "Tell me exactly what you're thinking, Donald."

"Well, I have to wonder if Doug Hall fenced those antiques for everyone else the way he did for Adam Hounslow — with or without their permission. I don't suppose we'll know until he's caught. But I felt certain you would want to know."

"And you're right, Donald. I only wish I had called you sooner." The line was silent for another moment before Malcolm spoke again. "Donald? There's something else I need you to do right away."

21

By the time Sheriff Hounslow and Deputy Peterson reached the small boarding house where Doug Hall's car had been seen, the Grantsville police, under the command of Captain Louis Bly, had already raided it.

Doug Hall's car wasn't there. Neither was Doug Hall.

Hounslow flashed his badge and pushed past the Grantsville officers who were trying to calm the bewildered landlady in the front hall. Other patrolmen were interviewing tenants in the door-ways to their rooms. Louis Bly was at the top of the stairs and signaled for Hounslow to follow him.

"Sorry we couldn't wait for you. The call went out on the moni-tor, and I was afraid he might hear it and run. He was gone by the time we got here anyway." They entered Hall's room, a sparsely decorated apartment with a bed, a dresser, and a sink.

"Looks like he plans to come back," Hounslow said, referring to the overnight case that sat open in the corner.

"We'll be here if he does," Bly confirmed.

Hounslow knelt next to the case. "Anything in here except clothes?"

"A toothbrush," Bly answered. "Oh, and those receipts. I was about to look through them when they said you'd arrived."

Hounslow picked up the small bundle of papers wrapped

with a rubber band and flipped through them. "These are receipts, all right. From antique shops in the area."

"Hall buys antiques?"

"Apparently he's been selling them." The bill of sale for his
father's shaving kit, ring, and photo was included. The rest of
them had familiar names written on them — all names of people
Hounslow had talked to at the retirement center.

"Selling them legitimately, or is he a fence for stolen
antiques?"

Hounslow suddenly realized that he didn't know. What if his
father had given Hall permission to sell those family treasures?
What if *all* the people at the center had? To Hounslow's trained
nose, it smelled like a scam of some sort. But what was the
scam? If those elderly folks had handed over their heirlooms to
Doug Hall, why would they do it?

"I'm sorry, Richard," Bly said. "I don't see anything here that
helps us with your father."

"It helps," Hounslow said as he stood up.

"How?"

"That's what I'm about to find out."

22

Somewhere over a very dark Frederick, Maryland, Malcolm's plane engines roared. Malcolm stared vacantly into the night sky. Jeff was buckled into the passenger seat, balancing on his lap the many pages contained in the two reports they'd been given by Detective White. A tiny reading lamp illuminated them.

"What are you doing?" Malcolm asked above the plane noise.

"Just killing time. I thought something might jump out at me if I looked long enough," Jeff replied. "Do you have any good ideas about what's going on?"

"I have plenty of theories," Malcolm said, "but nothing I can call a good idea."

"Same here."

"Let's think crazy for a little while, okay?" Malcolm suggested. For Malcolm and Jeff, thinking crazy was a common exercise. It meant letting go of conventional ideas and considering the implausible — even the impossible.

"First, let's allow that Fawlt Line really is sitting on some kind of time fault. That's how Elizabeth slipped through. So did King Arthur. Maybe Adam did too. But there's a problem."

"What kind of problem?" Jeff asked.

"According to Sheriff Hounslow, everything indicates that Adam went through *on purpose*. Detective White said essentially the same thing about McInery and Finney. It's as if their disappearances weren't accidents at all. They were planned. But how — and why?"

"I thought that's what we were trying to figure out," Jeff observed.

"It is. But to get the right answers, we have to come up with the right questions. So … let's ask ourselves: what if all these missing people *planned* to disappear?"

Jeff turned another couple of pages. "Then I have to wonder where they disappeared *to*. Is it some scheme to give them new identities and false passports so they can all sunbathe in Latin America somewhere?"

"Maybe. But why did they all disappear in historical sites? And why did they sell their personal belongings?"

"I give up. Why?"

"Beats me."

They flew on in silence for a while. Jeff continued to rifle through the pages, checking and double-checking bits of information.

Malcolm sighed. "I can't believe that Adam Hounslow is sun-bathing in Latin America. It doesn't make sense. To go to all this trouble, someone like Adam would want to go somewhere completely different. Somewhere that would do more than just let him escape."

"Like where?"

"If you were elderly, where would you want to go?" Malcolm asked.

Jeff thought about it for a minute. "If I were old and could go anywhere — anywhere at all — I'd probably want to go some-where that would make me feel young again."

"Yes!" Malcolm said. "Of course you would. You'd want to go back in time to being a young man!"

"We *are* talking crazy."

"That's the idea of this exercise," Malcolm reminded him.

"What if Adam Hounslow figured out how to slip through time on purpose? What if he found a door, a way to go back through the time fault? Is that why he surrounded himself with his personal heirlooms? Were they the key to open the door somehow?"

Jeff scratched his head. "Okay. I'll play along. I can understand something like that happening in Fawlt Line because Fawlt Line is weird. But Boston? Baltimore? Annapolis?"

"Historic towns with historic buildings. Maybe people like McInery and Finney figured out how to open the doors to other times, just as Adam Hounslow did."

"I can't believe that so many people would figure out a trick like that," Jeff said.

"Maybe they didn't figure it out. Maybe that's where Hall fits in."

Jeff shook his head. "How could someone like Hall come up with an idea like that?"

"I was only a kid when I started thinking about time travel."

"Yeah, but thinking about time travel is one thing, actually figuring out how to do it is another. I can't believe that Doug — " Jeff suddenly stopped himself. A chill went up his spine.

Malcolm glanced over at his nephew. "What's wrong?"

Jeff was staring at the sheets on his lap. "Incredible."

"What?"

"Doug Hall didn't do it alone," Jeff said softly.

Malcolm couldn't hear him over the hum of the plane's engine. "What did you say?"

Jeff spoke louder. "There's a list of people here who were living at the Arundel Nursing Home where Doug worked."

"And?"

"Mr. Betterman was there too."

At a quarter to ten, Elizabeth was idly pacing around Malcolm's den. She pulled one or two books from the shelves, glanced at them, and put them back. Mrs. Packer had fallen asleep in front of the TV. Had the housekeeper remembered to call the security guard at the Village? In fifteen minutes, something was going to happen at the Fawlt Line Cinema. Would the guard check it out?

Maybe nothing would happen at all. Maybe Frieda Schultz's note wasn't a cryptic cry for help, but just an innocent reminder to herself — like a "to do" list.

Yeah, right.

Elizabeth gazed at the sleeping Mrs. Packer, who now snored softly.

I wish Jeff and Malcolm would hurry up and get back. Then they could go investigate the cinema together. But there wasn't a chance they'd be back in time. And there might not be anything to investigate anyway.

But every instinct in Elizabeth's body said that Mrs. Schultz's note was a cry for help. She was trying to tell them that something important was going to take place at ten o'clock this very night.

Elizabeth took a step toward the sleeping figure. "Mrs. Packer?" she said softly.

The housekeeper didn't stir.

Why wake her up? Elizabeth asked herself. The cinema was less than a mile away. She knew the path to get there — straight across the meadow and through the small stretch of woods. She and Jeff had walked it a hundred times. She even knew how to open the private door Malcolm had put in the fence. Jeff had shown her. So why not go?

Because I'm scared, that's why, she thought.

"Mrs. Packer?" Elizabeth said softly.

Mrs. Packer didn't move.

It's silly to wake her up, Elizabeth thought. She had to overcome her fear. It was irrational. She'd just slip into the Village to see if anything was going on at the cinema and slip out again. What could possibly happen?

With a final glance at Mrs. Packer, Elizabeth opened the door to the patio and crept out into the night.

○ ○ ○

The Fawlt Line Cinema — with a marquee announcing the premiere of *It Happened One Night* — was situated on an unfinished street in the Village that would eventually be dedicated to the 1930s. It was dark and deserted. For a moment, Elizabeth felt as if she had slipped through a different kind of fault and wound up in a gangster movie. She shivered and paused a few yards from the cinema's front door.

If something was going on, walking through the front door wouldn't be a smart thing to do, so Elizabeth turned and followed the alley behind the cinema to the back door. It was unlocked. She turned the handle carefully so as not to make a lot of noise, but it creaked defiantly. Elizabeth got it open wide enough to slip through into a gray darkness. Dull-red safety lights were on, giving off enough of a glow for her to see that she was in a hallway. An excited voice echoed in another part of the building. Elizabeth tiptoed up the hall toward the sound.

A light through a break in the wall caught her eye. She peeked through and saw that she was alongside the stage curtain with the movie screen. Beyond the edge of the stage, a group of people she recognized from the retirement center sat in a semicircle under a bald light, facing Mr. Betterman in his wheelchair.

So, it was a secret meeting after all, she thought as her heart beat faster. Mr. Betterman gestured wildly as he spoke. Obviously, he was the leader of this little club. She felt relieved to be proven right in her suspicions of the man, but it didn't comfort her. It meant only that he was probably as dangerous as she always thought he was.

Elizabeth crept up the hallway until she came to a flight of stairs and an old sign pointing to the balcony. That would be a perfect vantage point to hear what Mr. Betterman was saying, she thought, and cautiously climbed the stairs.

Her father was right about the cinema. Even though it wasn't completely set up, it was ornately decorated with thick curtains, tassels, and gold trim that adorned the walls with swirling patterns. Elizabeth crawled along the dust-laden floor, through the unattached, disheveled chairs, to the edge of the balcony. On her knees, she slowly peeked over the railing, the smell of old wood filling her nostrils. The balcony gave her a perfect view of Betterman and his group, but they couldn't see her unless they knew to look for her — she hoped. She could hear Mr. Betterman more clearly now as his voice echoed powerfully around her.

"We've all been waiting years for this!" he said. "Gone are the days of praying for a miracle — waiting for those impossible, near-perfect circumstances for us to travel through time. No more sneaking around old haunts, buildings, and shops. Malcolm Dubbs has given us the perfect passage. Fawlt Line is the perfect place at the perfect time!"

Betterman spoke like a preacher. Even though he was a hunched-over old man in a wheelchair, the excitement he displayed made him seem younger somehow.

"Tonight is the night of miracles. Tonight all our hard work and sacrifice will be fulfilled. The words are on your lips, the keys are in your hands ... the door to a better place ... a better time ... awaits. Tonight you will reclaim your lost youth. Now you can say good-bye to twisted, arthritic bodies, ravaged by age. Return to your best days, your best health!"

Elizabeth tried to imagine how men and women so old and wise could believe such nonsense. Yet there they were: a small, elderly group who sat like wide-eyed children beholding a magician.

"Are there doubters?" he challenged them. "Then learn from Adam Hounslow! Where do you think he is now? He believed, and now he is there! Do you need more case histories? Look at the files and names I showed you. Where do you think they went? They went back to their youth — their paradise. The police couldn't find them. How could they?"

Elizabeth closed her eyes. What was he saying? Adam Hounslow went back in time? Had Mr. Betterman figured out how to send people back in time to better days? Was it possible?

"This is my gift to you," he said gently. "I spent every day of every year of my life in this time piecing it all together, while many called me insane. Even when they labeled me an amnesiac, I kept the faith. I knew who I was!"

Her skin crawled, and she wrapped her arms around herself to fight the uneasy feeling that was growing inside of her. *No, it can't be.* He was saying the same things she said when she was trapped in that other time. They said she was insane. They said she was an amnesiac. And she had to cling to the belief that she wasn't someone called Sarah. She was Elizabeth. She clenched her fists at the memory. *I am Elizabeth.*

Again, she saw Mr. Betterman as he had appeared in her dream. *I know who you are*, he had said, *Sarah.*

Betterman's tone built to a fevered pitch. "They had no idea, those fools. I knew that other times existed. I knew that there was a way to get back. But this was my purgatory, I realized. It doesn't have to be yours! There is a way out, and I will help you if you believe. Adam made it out. Now you will too." He pointed at them. "Are there any doubters now? Are there? Well, if you won't believe my words — if you won't believe the testimony of Adam — then believe this!"

As his words resounded throughout the building, Mr. Betterman leapt to his feet and victoriously pushed the wheelchair aside. The small group gasped as Elizabeth grabbed the railing to steady herself. *He can walk! The wheelchair* was *a fake after all!*

A buzz of comments and loud whispers went through the group, but Betterman wasn't finished with his presentation. "Tonight we strip away the facades, we rid ourselves of these feeble outer garments. Tonight we become our true selves!"

With one hand he grabbed his hat and slid it off. The wild hair came off with it to reveal short salt-and-pepper-colored hair. Elizabeth's eyes grew wider as a picture she'd been trying to form in her mind started taking shape.

Then he pulled off his beard, mustache, and sunglasses. He tilted his face toward the light and laughed like a much younger man.

Elizabeth put both fists against her mouth to stifle the scream rising in her throat. The picture was complete. She now knew why she thought she'd recognized him before. It was Crazy George.

She stumbled backward, narrowly grabbing a chair before it toppled.

"Go now!" he commanded them, like Moses leading the children of Israel. "You know what to do. Go to your destiny!"

Elizabeth fought back tears and tried to calm her palpitating heart.

No, it wasn't Crazy George. *It couldn't be,* her overloaded mind told her. Crazy George was a good man. He'd saved her life. He wouldn't have returned to this time to become so evil. No, it *looked* like Crazy George, but it wasn't. *It couldn't be.*

Her head throbbed as she tried to sort through the hows and whys. Just as Sarah was her time-twin and they'd swapped places, Mr. Betterman must be the time-twin for Crazy George. It had to be! Crazy George was trapped in the other time, but no one knew what had become of *his* time-twin. It had never occurred to Elizabeth to wonder where his time twin was.

Taking several deep breaths, Elizabeth tried to calm herself. She had to call someone — anyone. It wasn't right. Did those poor, misguided old people really understand what they were doing or where they were going? How could Betterman be sure where — or when — he was sending them? They had to be stopped. Elizabeth had to get out of there and tell somebody.

She quickly crawled back to the doorway to the hall and stood up.

Doug Hall stepped out of the shadows and blocked her path.

"Hello, Elizabeth." He leered. "Or should I call you Sarah?"

24

"Does the phrase 'obstruction of justice' mean anything to you?" Sheriff Hounslow barked at Mrs. Kottler. He had driven straight to the retirement center from the boarding house in Grantsville. Along the way, he received a message from Malcolm Dubbs that Betterman was definitely linked to the case and needed to be detained.

"Please, Sheriff," Mrs. Kottler said, moving in front of him as they walked quickly down the hallway. "The residents are traumatized as it is. Can't you wait until morning? You'll wake everyone up!"

"Waking some of them up is exactly what I have in mind — starting with Betterman! Now get out of my way."

She hovered in front of him. "I know what you're thinking, but — "

Hounslow stopped in his tracks. "Bob!"

Deputy Peterson, who'd been trying to keep up, joined them. "Yes, sir?" he panted.

"Get her out of my way," he said.

"Yes, sir." With surprising speed and strength, the deputy stepped in front of Mrs. Kottler, his hand on his nightstick.

"Now, wait just a minute — " Mrs. Kottler protested, but didn't try to move around him.

"If she causes any trouble, arrest her," Hounslow shouted as he continued down the hall.

It didn't take him very long to realize that he was on a wild goose chase. Betterman wasn't in his room, nor were the other ten people who had sold their belongings through Doug Hall.

"Where are they?" Sheriff Hounslow demanded when he returned from his search.

Mrs. Kottler blinked innocently. "Aren't they in their rooms?"

Hounslow pointed a finger at her. "Mrs. Kottler, I hope you're not involved in this. If I find out you that are ..." The implied threat hung between them.

She cleared her throat nervously. "Now that you mention it ... I believe some of the residents decided to take a drive in the center van. They do that sometimes, you know. I think Mr. Betterman may have been among them. Who else were you looking for?"

"Mrs. Kottler," the sheriff said in a low growl, "you'd better tell me *now* where they went. After that, I suggest you call your lawyer."

25

Doug Hall tore a strip of tassel from the stage curtain and tied Elizabeth's hands behind her back. She struggled until Betterman slapped her across the face. The sting brought tears to her eyes.

"I'm sorry, Sarah," Betterman said in earnest. "But if you don't behave, we're going to have a real problem on our hands."

Except for the three of them, the cinema was now empty. The retirement center residents had gone outside to do whatever Betterman had instructed them to do.

"I'm not Sarah," Elizabeth said.

Betterman smiled sympathetically at her. "You don't have to play that game with me. I know who you really are. You're Sarah Bishop. I knew your family in the *real* Fawlt Line — across the chasm of time. I worked with your father. You look a lot like your mother, actually."

Elizabeth winced as Doug gave the tassel a final tug to make sure it was secure. "You didn't know my family. You knew Sarah's. Haven't you figured it out? She's my time twin. Just like you have a time twin that you switched with when you came over. I met him. They called him Crazy George because everyone in that other time thought he was *you*. That's your name, isn't it? *George* Betterman?"

"Yes, it's my name," he said bitterly. "They kept calling me

Charles. They insisted that I agree and said it over and over again. 'Repeat after me: you're Charles Richards,' they'd say."

Elizabeth gasped. "*Charles Richards?*"

"Some woman I didn't know claimed to be my wife. Kids I'd never laid eyes on before kept calling me *daddy*." He let out a derisive laugh. "They said I was a *farmer*, of all things! Well, I told them what they could do with Charles Richards and his life. I was having no part of it. I was George Betterman, and no quack doctor was going to tell me otherwise."

"You were right!" Elizabeth said. "You are George Betterman, and Charles Richards is living in that other time. *Your* time. You switched places!"

"No kidding," Betterman said, but Elizabeth couldn't tell if he believed her or not. "Funny, isn't it? I just learned that if I'd agreed to be Charles Richards, I might've been wealthy. He owned all the land the old folks' home is sitting on."

Doug laughed. "What would you have done with the wife and kids?"

"I shudder to think of it," Betterman chuckled. Then he clapped his hands. "Okay, back to business."

"What business?" Elizabeth asked. "Don't you see? If you're George Betterman from that other time, then — "

"Shut up!" he shouted. "I don't want to hear anymore. Do you think I've spent my life here in vain? I *know* what happened to me. And I know what will happen tonight."

"Do you really? Have you really figured out how to transport people through time?"

"That remains to be seen," he said.

"Do you have any idea where — or when — you're sending those people?"

"To paradise," he said.

Elizabeth scowled at him. "Or to the *other* Fawlt Line — where they'll be treated like amnesiacs — or crazy people. Just like I was. Just like you were when you got *here*. They'll still be old. They won't be any happier. Why would you do that to them?"

"You don't know anything," he said. "They have the incantations; they have their trinkets. This is the pinnacle of time transference — to go to the places of their dreams where they will find youth and happiness again. Gone are the aches and pains of age. In these buildings, generously assembled by Malcolm Dubbs, they will stand at the doorway to time, say the words I've given to them, offer the meager souvenirs we've cleverly placed for them, and then step through."

"To *what*?" Elizabeth asked as she imagined the residents moving like zombies through the Village to their assigned buildings, their doorways. "Step through to *when*? Who knows what's out there. You don't. You *can't*. Not all doors lead to a better place. Please, Mr. Betterman, stop them."

Betterman wagged a finger at her. "Oh, don't be such a party pooper, Sarah. They'll go to a better place — or die trying." He laughed again.

At that moment, Elizabeth knew she was dealing with a madman.

"In fact," he said, "you and I should also make that trip across time. What do you say, Sarah? Shall we go home now?"

"No," Elizabeth cried out, then screamed as Hall lifted her to her feet. "No!"

26

Malcolm phoned Mrs. Packer as soon as he and Jeff landed at the Fawlt Line Airport. The first thing he learned was that Elizabeth had left the house.

He put his hand over the receiver and turned to Jeff. "Elizabeth left the cottage and didn't go home. Any idea where she might be now?"

Jeff's shook his head. "What time did she leave?"

Malcolm asked Mrs. Packer, then turned back to Jeff. "Around ten o'clock."

"I'll bet she's in the Village — at the old cinema."

Malcolm looked puzzled. "Why would she ...?" Then he remembered. "Mrs. Schultz's note! We're on our way."

He listened to Mrs. Packer again, then groaned. "Call security again right away and see if they've found anything ... You didn't? ... Just call them *now*, Mrs. Packer. Also, call Donald Nelson and tell him I'll meet him at the front gate. He knows what it's about."

Malcolm hung up the phone and moved quickly toward the Jeep.

"What's going on?" Jeff demanded.

"Everything. And I'm afraid Elizabeth's in the middle of it. Mrs. Packer said Hounslow called five minutes ago. He's going to the Village. Something to do with Mr. Betterman."

Donald Nelson was waiting for Malcolm and Jeff when they screeched to a halt at the front gate of the Village.

"Hello, Donald," Malcolm said as he climbed out of the Jeep. "Where is everyone?"

Donald rolled his eyes. "Sheriff Hounslow came in barking orders at everybody in sight. He sent his men and all the security guards to search the Village for Betterman and Doug Hall."

"They're both here?" Jeff asked.

"Hounslow seems to think so. I believe he persuaded the woman who runs the retirement center to confess, and she said — "

Jeff pressed his hand against his forehead. "Mrs. Kottler's in on this?"

"I'm only telling you what I heard."

"I'm going to the cinema," Jeff announced, running off.

Malcolm turned to Donald. "Did you do what I asked?"

"As best I could in the time I had."

"That'll have to do. Let's go." Malcolm strode into the Village.

✪ ✪ ✪

Jeff was nearly tackled and shot three times by police and security guards as he raced through the Village toward the cinema. He shouted where he was going and why and, before he knew it, had five men running with him. When they reached the cinema, the door was standing open and Hounslow was already inside.

"They aren't here," the sheriff said from the center of the auditorium. In his hand he held a wig, cap, sunglasses, and a beard. "I assume this is what's left of Betterman."

"Have you seen Elizabeth? Has anyone seen Elizabeth?" Jeff asked anxiously.

Hounslow shook his head, then yanked the walkie-talkie from his belt and asked for a report from around the Village.

Deputy Peterson informed him that they'd rounded up half a dozen folks from the retirement center, but they hadn't seen

Elizabeth. He also said they had found a service entrance gate unlocked and open.

"That's how the van from the retirement center got in — and probably got out again," Hounslow said.

"Then where did they go? They have Elizabeth with them!" Jeff shouted.

Hounslow clicked the button on his walkie-talkie. "Okay, guys, keep searching the Village, but I want a detail of men to hit the road. That retirement center van is headed somewhere, and I want it found. It's likely the suspects have Elizabeth Forde with them. And somebody get me a helicopter from the Frostburg police!"

Jeff dashed out of the building.

Hounslow looked at his officers. "What were all those old folks doing here? What were they up to?"

None of his men answered him.

✿ ✿ ✿

Malcolm and Donald stepped cautiously into the dimly lit farmhouse. It was on the outer edge of the Village and had been built to capture a lifestyle known to most Midwestern farmers from the turn of the century.

"Hello?" Malcolm called out.

His voice echoed throughout the house.

"You're sure this was one of them?" Malcolm asked Donald.

"Positive," he answered. "Doug Hall sold several boxes of things on behalf of the Sawyer family. They were designated for this house. I believe the Sawyers were farmers when — "

Malcolm held up a hand for him to be quiet. He had heard a noise in the next room. Now Donald heard it too. It was the sound of a man whimpering. Malcolm turned on a light in what would have once been a family room. Tiffany lamps, wing-backed chairs, full bookcases, and a player piano sat atop a deep red Persian carpet. A wizened old man sat in the corner, half-hidden by an end table and one of the chairs.

"Mr. Sawyer?" Malcolm said softly. "Are you all right?"

The man wept uncontrollably, his face buried in his hands. "They're not here."

"What are not here?"

"My *things*," he sobbed. "They were supposed to be here. How can I go back if they aren't here? I've said the words over and over again, but they're no good without my things."

"I had Mr. Nelson collect all of your things, Mr. Sawyer. He collected the belongings of everyone from the retirement center."

"But why?" the old man pleaded. "Don't you see? I can't go back without them. It won't work. Don't you understand? Please bring them back. Betterman promised that I'd go through time if I had my things and said the words."

Malcolm and Donald exchange a sad look. "Betterman is a liar, Mr. Sawyer," Malcolm said.

"No ... he can't be. We all believed him. He sent Adam back. He could do the same for us. He promised."

"How much did you all pay Betterman for this?" Malcolm asked gently.

The old man looked up at him helplessly and confessed, "All we had."

27

A police car flew past with its lights flashing and siren screaming.

"All clear?" Betterman asked.

Doug leaned forward to check the road in both directions. "All clear." He started up the motor and guided the van back onto the road.

Betterman turned in the passenger seat and addressed Elizabeth, who was tied up and stretched out on the floor. "It won't be long now," he said.

She grunted through the silver tape over her mouth.

Doug turned onto an unpaved road. The van bounced along, and Elizabeth grunted and groaned with each bump.

"I liked your family, Sarah," Betterman said. "Good people. I thought of them a lot when I came to this time. They were some of the folks I missed. So you can imagine my surprise when I found out that you were here too. I was delighted. Wasn't I delighted, Doug?"

"You were," Doug replied.

Betterman turned to face her again. "Ever since I got here, I've been studying time travel and what some people called 'weird phenomena.' It was sort of a natural interest to me since I'd come from another time. Nobody believed me though. They just wanted to lock me up and throw away the key. In fact, Doug here was the only one who believed me. We were at that Happy Dale Sanitarium, weren't we?"

Doug nodded. "Uh-huh."

"It was Doug who happened to see a tiny article in some cheesy tabloid about the mysterious disappearance of a girl in a strange little town called Fawlt Line. She disappeared right out of her bathtub, the article said. Then the writer pointed out that this was the same Fawlt Line where several other bizarre things had happened over the last fifty years. That tabloid writer meant it as a joke, I know, but it sure got my interest. Do you remember, Doug?"

"I remember." Doug smiled. "It was all you talked about."

"I thought, We're going to have to check out old Fawlt Line and those bizarre occurrences. It took some doing."

"A lot of money," Doug put in.

"That's right. I got a couple of interns at the hospital to tell me everything they knew about the girl in a coma who was supposed to be Elizabeth. Later, I heard things about her disappearing right under the doctor's nose. Then a cop told me about all the other peculiar things that happened. He even got me a classified file from the police station that had a full statement from you and Jeff and Malcolm. As soon as I read the name Sarah Bishop, I knew. I put two-and-two together and knew that you were Sarah — only they'd brainwashed you into believing you were Elizabeth. Better than that, I realized that Fawlt Line was the town for me."

A tear slid down Elizabeth's nose and onto the worn carpet.

Doug brought the van to a halt and got out. Betterman climbed back to help Elizabeth sit up. "Your father would be proud of how you turned out," he said.

Doug opened the side door, and Betterman guided Elizabeth out. She hit the gravel on wobbly knees and looked around for anything that might tell her where they were.

She saw a ramshackle old building, the wooden boards pulled

away from rusty nails. On the far end was what was left of a giant water-wheel. They had brought her to the Old Saw Mill.

"Great idea, huh?" Doug said.

"If I remember right, this is where you showed up after switching back and forth through time. So we figured it would be the best place for what we need to do. Didn't we, Doug?"

"Yep," Doug said.

Betterman smiled at her. "You've done me no end of good, Sarah. You and Malcolm. You're inspirations to me. I thought I had died and gone to heaven when I heard he was building his Historical Village. It was as if he'd done it just for me. I thought, *Here's a man with vision. A whole village with doorways into time. Perfect, absolutely perfect.* Take that tape off her mouth, will you, Doug?"

Doug gently removed the tape. "Is that better?"

"Yes," Elizabeth said breathlessly. "What are we doing here?"

"You'll see," Betterman said as he and Doug each took an elbow and escorted Elizabeth into the derelict wooden building. It was full of cobwebs and the smell of rotting wood and sawdust. Somewhere not far beyond the woods, they could hear the river splashing over the rocks.

"Memories, huh?" Doug said.

Elizabeth remembered, all right, and it sent a shiver of panic through her entire body. She had sworn to herself that she would never come back here. Not only because of what had happened before, but also because of what she feared could happen again. Now it seemed as if Betterman was going to make it happen.

She struggled against her captors, panic rising in her throat. "No, please, I don't want to be here. Take me away from here."

Betterman clicked his tongue at her. "Now don't fuss, Sarah. This is all for the best."

"I'm not Sarah!" Elizabeth shouted at him. "I'm Elizabeth! Sarah is in the other time where she belongs. I'm in this time where I belong! Cross over if you know how to, but don't take me with you!"

"Oh, now, you at least have to try," Betterman said. "How will we know if it really works unless we experiment on you? If you cross over, then maybe Doug and I can too."

"You and Doug?" Elizabeth asked, bewildered. "It doesn't work that way."

"It has to. What would I go back to if Doug doesn't come with me? Doug is the only family I have now."

"But what about my family? My life?"

"What about them? Good grief, Sarah, you haven't been here that long." Betterman signaled to Doug. "Tie her to the pole."

Doug pulled Elizabeth to a supporting pole in the center of the mill. He brought a stretch of cord out of his back pocket and secured her already-tied wrists to the beam.

Elizabeth glared at Doug. "It won't work if I'm tied up."

He kissed her on the cheek. "You're a clever girl. If I untie you, you'll figure out how to run away." Once he was certain she was secure, he turned to Betterman. "What now?"

"Let's say the words and see what happens."

"You're kidding."

"What have we got to lose? If it's going to work for anybody, it'll work for her."

"If you insist . . ." Doug stepped away from Elizabeth and stood next to Betterman. They faced her for a moment before closing their eyes.

"Please don't do this," Elizabeth said.

Betterman raised his arms. "Force of time, endless river, open door."

"I don't want to be sent to another time. Please, don't!"

"In time there is regeneration and rebirth," Betterman continued. "We seek it within ourselves. We seek it within time. Send now the force of time to take Sarah to her happiest time. Through the force of time, take her into that doorway. Take her ... and may the force be with her."

Elizabeth gasped — and then suddenly composed herself, staring at Betterman incredulously.

Doug chuckled. "May the force be with her?"

Betterman shrugged. "It seemed like the right thing to say. The old folks always liked it."

"Is this some kind of cruel joke?" Elizabeth asked angrily.

Betterman pondered the question. "Cruel? Maybe. A joke? Hardly. You see, I really do believe in time travel, but I've never been able to figure out how to master it. It's been an endless source of disappointment."

"Then what was all that 'crossing over' stuff?"

"You're going to cross over, all right," Betterman explained. "But not in the way you expected. In fact, you're going to join Adam."

"Adam? Adam Hounslow? Where is he?"

Doug hooked a thumb toward another part of the mill. "He's under a tarp in the back."

"Go get the boxes, Doug," Betterman said and the younger man obeyed.

Elizabeth's mouth was agape. "You mean Adam didn't go to another time? He's ... he's ... dead?"

"We didn't kill him on purpose. It was an accident," Betterman explained.

"What kind of accident?"

Betterman considered her for a moment and then smiled evilly. "I suppose I'm obligated to tell you. Don't the bad guys always spill the beans at the end of the movie? Otherwise, you'll never know, will you?"

"What kind of accident?" Elizabeth asked again.

"You see, the plan was supposed to be simple. While visiting the Village on opening day, Adam would send his son off on some errand, then go into the mining row house where he'd say the words and disappear to another time — or so he thought."

"But you knew he wouldn't," said Elizabeth. "Still, you decided to use him as your proof to the other old folks that what you were saying was true."

Betterman nodded. "It was easier than we thought. We put up a quick 'Do Not Enter' sign on the front of the row house, used a little chloroform, dropped Adam into my wheelchair and dressed him up to look like me."

Elizabeth was astonished. "I saw him! I saw Doug wheel him out! And it didn't make sense to me why Doug would be pushing your *electric* wheelchair."

Doug had returned with some boxes and said to Elizabeth. "You'll forgive me for not saying hello when we were leaving the Village. I was afraid you might want to make conversation and realize that the man in the wheelchair wasn't Betterman."

Elizabeth directed herself to Betterman. "So you just walked out, knowing no one would recognize you without your cap, sunglasses, and hair?"

"I was afraid that you would recognize me, but you'd already left."

Elizabeth thought about it a moment. "You walked out. That's how you got the dirt and grass on your shoes."

"Yet another close call, thanks to you," Betterman said appreciatively.

"I thought you got dirt on your shoes because you had buried Adam's stuff in the woods."

"You were wrong about that," Betterman said. "It was Doug who buried Adam's belongings the night before. The plan was then to bring Adam here and keep him locked up until we got the rest of the money from the old fogies at the center."

"Quite a coup, getting the sheriff's father to buy into the scheme," Doug said proudly. "It gave us a lot of credibility with the doubters."

"What happened to him?" Elizabeth asked.

"Doug brought him here, but to our surprise he had died en route. Maybe we gave him too much chloroform, or it triggered a heart attack or something. Sad. Same thing happened to Frieda Schultz. But that was on purpose, of course — the woman was going to ruin our entire plan. We moved her pills and gave her the scare of her life. Unfortunately, she started wailing like a banshee. It wasn't our week, was it, Doug?"

Doug shook his head with mock sadness.

Elizabeth shook her head as she thought of the lives of Frieda and Adam. What a terrible waste. "All of this for a scam."

"Not just a scam," Betterman protested. "A *great* scam. We've been doing it all over the country. Besides, what's wrong with giving old folks a little hope in their dreary lives?"

"Plenty, when people get murdered or — "

Betterman held up a hand. "All right, all right. Don't get preachy. It's a risk of the trade and small compensation for the life *I* lost when I switched from my time to this one. Anyway, it was nice while it lasted."

"While it lasted?"

"This was our last hurrah," he said. "One doesn't inadvertently kill a sheriff's father and expect to go unpunished. Doug and I are moving on to greener pastures. Aren't we, Doug?"

Doug had left and now returned with another couple of boxes. "This is the last of it."

"What happens now?" Elizabeth asked.

Betterman flicked his hand at the boxes. "Oh, these boxes have all the evidence about our little program. By the time the police find you and Adam and the boxes, we'll be long gone."

"South America," Doug added. "Or maybe Spain. I've been practicing my Spanish."

"Or Switzerland," said Betterman. "I've heard that Basel is very nice — and conveniently located on the border of Germany and France."

Elizabeth scowled. "You're going to leave me here?"

"Yes, my dear," Betterman said. "What happens to you from this point forward isn't my concern." He walked out.

Doug leaned close to her face. His breath smelled of mint. "We could have made beautiful music together," he said, brushing his lips against hers. *"Buenos noches."*

"Don't leave me here like this!" Elizabeth called after him. "Please!"

Betterman suddenly poked his head back in. "Do you want to come with us?"

"No!" she shouted.

He grinned. "Then — good-bye, *Sarah.*"

⚙ ⚙ ⚙

Doug climbed into the van, started the engine, put it into gear, then jumped out again to watch as the van propelled itself over the embankment and down into the woods. It crashed head-on against a tree and died. He then ran over to a small blue car where Betterman was waiting in the passenger seat. "Ready?" he asked.

Betterman drummed his fingers on the dashboard and frowned. "I'm thinking twice about leaving her there. What if the police find everything before we get out of the country?"

"Good point."

"You better take care of it."

Doug got out of the car. He went around to the trunk and pulled out a gas can, then walked to one of the mill's walls and splashed the liquid on the sides. He lit a match and placed it against the wood. It went up fast.

Back in the car, he said, "That old dry wood will be gone in no time at all."

Betterman smiled and cocked an ear to something he heard in the sky above. "Let's get out of here."

28

Fred Danziger, a helicopter pilot from the Frostburg police, had been watching the road for a white van. The call came in as he was ending his shift to go home. He was tired and annoyed and muttering curses at Sheriff Hounslow, Fawlt Line, and whatever bad guys down there had started the kind of trouble that required his services. "Watch for a white passenger van with printing on the side," was all he knew.

Small towns, he snorted to himself. *What happened? Did somebody steal Grandma's quilt?* Route 40 was clear. So was the bypass. He circled around and saw a glimmer of moonlight reflect off the small river below. He couldn't remember the river's name — or if it even had one. He had a vague notion that it was once used for mining or lumber mills.

He yawned, then did a double take as he realized that the moonlight on the river had taken on a red-and-yellow glow. It wasn't moonlight at all. It was the reflection of a fire that seemed to be working its way up the side of a large wooden building. A mill, he guessed. He hit the spotlight to confirm that the building really was on fire.

Another pinprick of light caught his eye, and he trained the spotlight on the road running away from the mill. A small car was speeding away from the scene.

Fred grabbed his radio microphone.

○ ○ ○

Elizabeth twisted around to see if there was any way to undo the knots on her wrists or pull away from the pole. Doug had done a thorough job. Her hands were going to sleep. She suddenly stopped and sniffed the air. The thick smoke that curled ribbon-like through the cracks in the wall told her all she needed to know.

She screamed, but knew there was no one around to help.

Twisting and squirming until her arms and back ached, she worked her wrists back and forth. The rope and cord cut through her skin. She again turned her head to get a clearer view of how she'd been tied up. Double, even triple knots had her securely bound.

The fire hissed and crackled outside, and something shifted above her. She was terrified to see that the flames had moved to the roof. The smoke and heat were thick inside now. Elizabeth began to cough uncontrollably.

She looked down again at the ropes, the cord, and the pole to see if there was anything at all that might set her free. *God, help me*, she prayed. *Help me.*

She spotted part of a nail sticking out of the pole, just a few inches beneath her bonds. Using all of her weight, she pushed downward, hoping to catch the ropes or the cords on the nail itself. Maybe if she rubbed back and forth enough, the nail would fray the ropes so she could break free. She'd seen heroes do it on television. The ropes cut into her wrists more as she pressed down with all of her might. Beads of sweat appeared on her forehead, and the feeling was completely gone from her hands. She coughed harder as the smoke poured in.

I won't burn to death, she thought glibly. *The smoke will kill me first.*

Suddenly she wished that she *could* transfer to another time. It looked like her only escape.

The fire was wildly alive now, and pieces of wood were falling down from the roof. Elizabeth frantically scraped the ropes against the rusted nail. Her eyes teared up and her coughing became more violent. *How long will it take?* she wondered as her struggle with the nail weakened. She had a different struggle now: the struggle to stay conscious.

Oh, God, somebody must have seen the flames. Somebody must be on their way. But will they make it in time?

She put all of her strength into another jerk at the ropes and the nail. Then another. Then another. Blackness closed in, and she slumped against the pole. Her legs gave out, and the tightness of the ropes twisted her arms agonizingly upward, but she didn't notice.

She was barely conscious when a figure moved across the floor, coming toward her through the smoke.

29

Fred Danziger's radio report brought an immediate response from all who heard it. The local fire engines were sent screaming to the Old Saw Mill. Hounslow ordered the helicopter to stay on the mysterious blue car until he and his men could intercept it farther down Route 40. Roadblocks were immediately set up. The chase was on to snag their prey.

"Faster, faster!" Hounslow shouted at his car. In the distance, he could see the blue car's taillights. The helicopter suddenly swooped in, washing the scene in white light. "Okay, that's it. Let's drive the fox to the hounds."

✿ ✿ ✿

Doug Hall swore and pounded the steering wheel. "It's not fair! It's not fair!"

"Just keep driving, son," Betterman said as he glanced back at the red-and-blue lights coming toward them in the darkness. The spotlight from the helicopter suddenly hit them again in a blinding flash. "We'll think of something."

They rounded a corner.

"Roadblock!" Doug shouted.

Betterman jerked around. The line of police cars with their flashing lights was about fifty yards ahead.

"What should we do? I can't ram them in this little matchbox," Doug said.

Betterman considered their options to the left and right. The woods were thick on both sides. "We can make a run for it. Hit the brakes," he said.

Doug began to slow down. "Are you sure?"

Hounslow's siren got louder as it came up behind them.

"I didn't say to slow down! I said *hit the brakes!*" With that, Betterman lifted his foot and thrust it down on top of Doug's on the brake pedal. The car screeched, lurching from side to side as it went into an uncontrollable skid.

✿ ✿ ✿

Hounslow swore as he slammed on his brakes. The car ahead swerved to the left, then skidded in a half circle. It spun another few degrees and tipped off the road onto the dirt shoulder. It dipped into a pothole and flipped onto its side. Hounslow had a moment's view of the undercarriage as the car flipped from its side onto its roof and careened toward the gully that lined the right side of the road. Sparks flew, metal shrieked. Off the pavement, the car hit the dirt and flipped yet again down to the edge of the woods.

Hounslow's vehicle also threatened to swerve as he wrestled for control. The antilock brakes kicked in and he brought the car to a sensible halt amidst the smell of burning rubber and smoke.

The sheriff shouted into his radio microphone. "Get an ambulance down here right away!" He leapt out of the car and raced to the tangled blue mess down the embankment. The turn signal flashed forlornly, like an appeal for help. The helicopter seemed to appear from nowhere, its spotlight starkly lighting the scene.

✿ ✿ ✿

Doug Hall was dazed. A thick line of blood appeared on his forehead and sent drops down his nose and cheeks. He looked over at the passenger side of the car. Betterman wasn't there.

"Betterman!" Doug called out. The seat was empty, but the

door was closed. The window was cracked, but still in place. Confused, Doug pulled himself out of the wreck. "Betterman!" he shouted, staggering around the car.

Hounslow reached Doug, holding his gun in both hands. "Don't move," he commanded as he crouched into a shooter's position.

Doug raised his hands. "No problem here."

"Where's your pal?"

"I don't know," Doug said, his eyes scanning the area.

"You don't know?" Hounslow challenged him. He quickly checked to make sure Betterman wasn't sneaking up behind him.

Doug collapsed onto the embankment and rubbed his face. *How could Betterman disappear?*

Hounslow began barking orders in his walkie-talkie. Doug heard some of the words — "search," "perimeter," "leapt or thrown from the car" — but Doug knew instinctively that they would never find George Betterman.

As the helicopter trained its spotlight on the scene and the rest of the police cars pulled up, Doug looked up at Hounslow, who gazed back at him with steely eyes, the sheriff's gun trained on his chest.

"Where is my father?" the sheriff demanded.

30

Opening the sliding glass door, George stepped out of his hotel room and onto the small ground floor patio. Above him, a neon sign buzzed. E-Z Rest Motel, it said.

This was his vacation, just as the hospital psychologist, Dr. Forbes, had suggested. It was all he could afford. Not a bad deal, all in all, with a heated pool and satellite television in every room.

George didn't care about those things. He came to the E-Z Rest because it sat on the piece of land that, in his time, was his. George figured that the swimming pool on the other side of the hedge was right where his little pond had been — in that other time.

From a nearby room he could hear the canned laughter of a sitcom on one of the televisions. In any time or world, canned laughter was a bad idea, he thought.

He pushed through the hedge and strolled aimlessly to the swimming pool. At this hour, no one was swimming. It was a little too cool for that. He went through the small metal gate and passed the diving board, walking along the edge, gazing down at the water. He stopped. He had a bizarre tingling feeling deep in his gut.

Something is going to happen.

Then he saw red, blue, and white flashing lights in the bottom of the pool. The water was still, and he looked up to make sure it wasn't simply reflecting the neon sign. It wasn't. There were flashing lights — like police car lights — at the bottom of the pool. George leaned over for a closer look. Suddenly, his head spun and that feeling in his gut became a jolt in his chest, as if someone punched him hard there. He lost his balance and fell into the water.

Not another heart attack.

He gasped, clawing at anything, trying to get his bearings. His hand banged against a metal ladder and he grabbed on. Thank God, he thought. He began to pull himself up, but his wet fingers slipped and his head crashed against the side of the pool as he plunged under the water again.

In a split second, he thought, *I knew something was about to happen, but I didn't think it might be my death.*

31

Len Sebastian, Fawlt Line's fire chief, put his hands on his hips and watched the Old Saw Mill tilt like a storm-tossed ship and collapse in a sea of fire. "We should've torn this place down years ago," he muttered to himself.

His squad of firemen blasted water from three different hoses at the flames.

"Chief, Hounslow's on the horn for you!" somebody shouted.

Sebastian leaned into his car and grabbed the radio. "Sebastian here."

"It's Hounslow. Did you find anybody?"

"Find anybody where?" he asked.

"In the Old Saw Mill? Were there any survivors?"

Sebastian looked at the flaming wreckage. His years of experience said that if people were inside, they couldn't have survived. "Well, Sheriff — "

He was interrupted by a shout. "Chief! Yo — Chief!"

"Hold on," Sebastian said. His man pointed toward the woods.

"I'll get back to you," he said and dropped the microphone. He ran in the direction of the woods and pushed through a group of his men. Sitting next to a tree, covered in a protective fire jacket, a girl cried and coughed. Next to her lay an old man. Two firemen raced toward them with first-aid kits.

Someone leaned over to Sebastian and said, "He's alive, but barely."

"Get an ambulance," Sebastian snapped. He walked over and knelt next to the girl. "Can you talk?"

She nodded, then coughed and cleared her throat. "Yes," she rasped.

"Who are you?"

"Elizabeth Forde," she whispered. Tears formed wavy lines down her soot-stained cheeks.

There was another commotion in the crowd as Jeff, then Malcolm, pushed their way through.

"Bits!" Jeff cried out and stumbled toward her, kneeling down to wrap his arms around her.

She leaned against him and lost whatever self-control was left. "He saved my life," she said through wrenching sobs and coughs.

"Who?"

"Adam Hounslow."

○ ○ ○

"I thought I was dead," Adam Hounslow told his son in a thin voice. "It was like a dream."

He was on a stretcher in the back of the ambulance, speeding for the hospital. The sheriff sat next to him. Adam was suffering from dehydration, the paramedic said. Some smoke inhalation too. Adam coughed softly.

"For once in your life, be quiet," Hounslow said.

"Don't talk to your father like that," Adam replied. He looked at his son with sunken eyes. "What if I don't make it to the hospital?"

"It'd be just like you to do that to me." Hounslow half smiled.

Adam swallowed hard. "Then you should know now."

"Know what?"

"Betterman and that Hall kid sold us a load of nonsense. They got us all worked up about going to a better place in time."

"I know, Dad," Hounslow said. "We got the whole story from some of your pals at the center."

"I wanted it, Richard. I wanted another life. That's why I agreed to be their guinea pig. But when I got to the mining house and they hit me with that chloroform, I knew it was a scam. I wanted to die right then and there. I didn't care anymore. To have hope — and lose it so quickly — it was more than I could take."

"Calm down, will you?" Hounslow said soothingly and stroked his father's matted hair.

Adam sniffled. "It was like those other times. I went deep inside myself."

"A self-induced coma, I think the doctors called it," Hounslow suggested.

"Whatever. All I know is I felt an emptiness like I'd never felt before. It was horrible. But I thought that's what death was like, so I figured I really had died. It was like a dream. Then I started coughing and figured that dead people don't cough. So I opened my eyes and there I was, all wrapped up. I thought I was in a coffin, Richard. I thought I was buried alive." He went into a coughing fit.

"Take it easy!" Hounslow said and put a restraining hand on his father's arm. "You're giving me the creeps. Just lie still."

"That's when I realized that I didn't want to be dead," Adam continued after he caught his breath again. "I wanted to live. So I punched a fist at the coffin lid, and it wasn't a coffin lid after all. It was a tarp. I fought my way out and saw that girl tied to the pole, and the building on fire, and there was no question about it. I wanted to live."

"You saved Elizabeth's life."

"Did I? Oh, well, that's nice. I'm glad."

Hounslow gazed at his father and saw a light in his eyes that he hadn't seen in a long time. "Dad ..."

"Yeah?"

"I was thinking ... I was wrong to make you move to that retirement center."

"Oh?"

"Yeah. Maybe you should move in with me."

A thin smile crossed Adam's face. "What — are you kidding? And give up Twister with Mrs. Kottler?"

Hounslow took his father's hand and laughed.

The radio on Hounslow's belt coughed at him. "Hey, Sheriff, are you there?"

"I'm here," he barked at the deputy.

"We've searched everywhere. There's no sign of Betterman."

"He has to be there somewhere."

"We've gone over every inch of the area — even farther than you'd said. He's gone."

"What'd he do, grow wings and fly? Keep looking."

"But — "

"*Keep looking*," Hounslow shouted. "We can't let this man get away."

Malcolm sat on a hard plastic chair in the corner of the emergency waiting room and stared at the worn green carpet. Elizabeth was somewhere on the other side of the double doors, being checked over by a doctor. Jeff was with her. Malcolm had called Elizabeth's parents, and they were on their way.

This was supposed to be the happy ending to this story, Malcolm thought, but it wasn't. Not yet. The news that George Betterman had disappeared was troubling.

By all accounts, Betterman was in the car with Doug Hall. When Hall had lost control of the vehicle, there was no time for Betterman to leap out — nor was he thrown. And even if one or the other had happened, the speed of the car would have made it virtually impossible for Betterman to run away from the scene.

So where did he disappear to?

"Malcolm?" Jeff called out.

Malcolm lifted his head. Jeff and Elizabeth came toward him, through the double doors and past the plastic chairs. They were holding hands. Elizabeth's face looked red and puffy, but she stood erect and strong.

Malcolm was on his feet. He hugged her gently. "Are you all right?"

"I'm fine," she replied in a scratchy voice.

"There's something you need to know," Jeff said.

Elizabeth coughed, then gestured for Jeff to speak.

Jeff nodded. "George Betterman is a time twin."

"What?" Malcolm asked, looking from Jeff to Elizabeth and back again.

"I recognized him," Elizabeth struggled to say. "The name."

"Without all his make-up, he looked exactly like Crazy George," Jeff said. "He came over from the other time. He admitted it. He's been here for years. But he refused to accept that he was mentally ill, like everyone had told him."

"Or an amnesiac," Elizabeth added.

"So he kept his own name."

Malcolm ran his fingers through his hair, his mind racing with this new piece of information. "That explains his disappearance. He must have switched back to his real time."

"Which means someone from that time has switched back over here," Jeff said.

Malcolm took a deep breath. "This is amazing. I wonder who switched over, or where he'll show up."

"We know who it is," Jeff said.

"You do?"

Elizabeth coughed again, then rasped, "It's Charles Richards."

Malcolm was stunned. He searched both faces to make sure it wasn't a joke. "Charles Richards," he repeated. He could hear his heart pounding in his ears. "Charles Richards is Betterman's time twin?"

"That's right," Jeff said, a hint of a smile on his face.

And then Malcolm remembered why he thought Betterman's name was so familiar. "I'm such an idiot," he said.

"What?" Jeff asked, puzzled.

"Betterman. The name is in my files on Charles Richards," Malcolm explained. "There was a doctor's report about a man who turned up, looking uncannily like Charles Richards. But he claimed his name was George Betterman and refused to acknowledge anything to do with Richards. He escaped, not to be heard from again."

"That fits with what Mr. Betterman said to me," Elizabeth whispered.

"Before he tried to kill you," Jeff added.

"That means . . ." Malcolm began to say, but found himself stammering and sputtering like an old English soldier in the movies. "He's back . . . Good heavens . . . We have to find him!"

"But where would he show up? The Old Saw Mill? The place where Betterman disappeared?" Jeff asked.

"No." Malcolm thought for a moment. "No. There's another possibility."

33

Under a starlit sky, George — or Charles Richards, as he was once known — sat on a wooden picnic table and gazed at the water. The moon danced upon the gentle waves. A nearby sign called it Richards Lake.

Funny, he thought, *we used to call it 'the pond.'* Someone had added a lot of water to it since he had last been here over three decades ago.

Taking his shirt in both hands, he wrung out the water. It dripped and splashed onto the cement block beneath the table. Then he brought part of it up and dabbed the scrape near his temple. It stung.

He turned, looking around yet again. The E-Z Rest Motel was gone. Behind him in the distance, the fluorescent lights of a large building held a steady glow. It looked like a hospital, he thought, but it stretched out on a single level and the movement of an occasional staff person dressed in white made him suspect it was some sort of retirement home.

If he squinted just a little, he could imagine that those lights belonged to the house he once called home — the place he had shared with his wife and children.

Dear God, he prayed, *have You brought me back?*

He had yearned for it for so many years that he now hesitated to believe it was true. Everything in his being told him it was, but he didn't dare allow the hope to well up within him just yet. There was so much he'd have to think about, so much to adjust to after all this time, so many questions.

He heard footsteps — soft, swooshing sounds — and inclined his gaze toward the sound. Three shadows moved his way, striding with purpose toward him. This was no casual evening stroll. They were coming for him.

He ought to be wary, he thought. Three strangers could mean him harm. Maybe he was trespassing, even though it was once his property.

Or, worse, they might be three people who will call him George, and then he'll know for certain that he hadn't returned to his own time. That would be crushing. It might even drive him crazy.

The three were now closer, and he could see that one was an older man with two young adults. Their faces were obscured by darkness as the moon ducked behind a cloud.

He mustered his courage. "Hello there," he called out in a friendly tone.

The moon emerged and Charles saw the three faces. A middle-aged man, a young man named David or Jeff, depending which time he was in. And then there was the attractive young woman who might be Sarah or Elizabeth.

He froze at the sight of them, holding his breath, aware of his dripping clothes. He wondered who he was to them.

"Crazy George?" the girl said. She was smiling. He stared at her, remembering that only Elizabeth had ever called him that.

"Mr. Charles Richards?" the older man said.

"Yes," he replied, and his hope — so cautiously contained — now exploded from its bonds. He stood up.

The man held out his hand. "Nice to see you again after all these years."

34

The charred remains of the Old Saw Mill seemed strangely peaceful under the blue morning sky. The twisted metal stairs leading to a second-floor office reminded Elizabeth of a child's pencil sketch — all jagged lines and blurry smudges. The blackened door stood open on its hinges and the shell beyond was nothing but broken black toothpicks. She could see the woods beyond.

Elizabeth shivered as a cool breeze swept through. She had come back to the site hoping to put a permanent end to this bad dream. She looked down at the bandages on her wrists. *Let it be over now*, she thought.

"Are you all right?" Jeff asked softly.

Elizabeth coughed and cleared her throat. The doctor said she'd be doing a lot of that over the next few days. "As well as can be expected."

Malcolm suddenly appeared from around a remaining corner of the building, stepping gingerly over the heap of rubble. He was wearing heavy boots and looked as though he should be fly-fishing, not walking around a burned-down building. "I found it!" he exclaimed and held something up.

A bird screeched indignantly from a tree nearby and flew off.

"What did you find?" Jeff called back.

Malcolm leapt from the last fallen beam and walked across the lot to them. "The ax Adam used to cut you loose, Elizabeth."

"Is that how he did it? I wasn't sure."

"I thought it'd be nice to have when we go visit him this afternoon."

Elizabeth looked thoughtfully at the wreckage. "I prayed for God to help me when I was inside there. I guess I expected him to make the ropes fall off. I didn't expect him to bring Adam Hounslow back."

Malcolm chuckled. "Looks like God answered two prayers. Yours and the sheriff's."

"Three," Elizabeth corrected him. "Don't forget Charles Richards."

They stood in silence for a moment until Elizabeth coughed again. "Do you think it's over?"

Baffled, Jeff and Malcolm looked at her.

She cleared her throat. "Now that the Old Saw Mill is gone and Charles Richards is back, is the door closed to that other time?"

Malcolm shrugged. "I don't know. Can anybody know for sure? Only God knows."

Elizabeth breathed deeply, wanting to believe it. "Okay."

"Although ..." Malcolm began, then paused.

"Although what?" Jeff asked.

"It makes me wonder about the Village."

"What about it?"

"Well, I've been thinking about George Betterman," Malcolm said. "Because of people like him, there are places in this world that can become centers of the wrong kinds of thinking — where the truth gets distorted into a terrible lie and false hope gets sold to the vulnerable. I built the Village as a testimony to history. Without realizing it, I may have opened new and very dangerous doors. That worries me. What's in the future for the Village, if it becomes the center of things that are misguided and evil?"

"But that could happen anywhere, to anything," Jeff said.

Elizabeth spoke quietly. "You always taught us that when people learn the truth, they're less susceptible to lies. Crooks like Mr. Betterman can only do what they do because people turn their backs on the truth. Isn't that how it works?"

Malcolm fixed his gaze on Elizabeth, pleased. "That's right. Sometimes we'll do just about anything when we're afraid, or we've lost hope, or we've forgotten how to appreciate our lives. But in God's truth, there is no fear. There's hope and life. Remembering that will always keep the Mr. Bettermans in their place."

"And maybe set the ones like Charles Richards free," Jeff suggested.

Malcolm suddenly glanced at his watch. "The Village opens in one hour, and I need to be there."

He turned and walked to his Jeep. Jeff touched Elizabeth's arm and started to follow. She paused for a moment to look back at the skeletal remains of the Old Saw Mill. The rubble, the twisted stairs, the shell of the office, and that door ... she had a feeling about that door. No, not a feeling. It was a small prayer.

"What's wrong?" Jeff asked, stopping to see what she was looking at.

"Wait," she whispered.

She watched as a breeze gently blew the door. It moved slightly — and then with a weary groan, it closed shut.

She closed her eyes gratefully. "Now it's over," she said.

35

Charles sat, cradling a cup of hot coffee in his hands. He could feel the heat pressing against his palms. Glancing at his fingernails, he thought, *Funny, I can't remember the last time my hands were this clean.* His white Oxford shirt and navy blue trousers were new and pressed.

"Well, Mr. Richards. This is amazing," Dr. Amos said pleasantly.

George looked up from his place in the guest chair and across the metal desk of the hospital's staff psychologist. There were short stacks of files between them.

"I've looked through all of Malcolm Dubbs' case files on you," Dr. Amos said. "Do you know that he's spent most of his life studying your case?"

Charles nodded. "We've talked about it." For hours, in fact. Some might say that Malcolm Dubbs was obsessed with his case. But it was understandable, as far as Charles was concerned. As the boy in Dr. Beckett's car, it must have been traumatic to see a man disappear right in front of him. "Malcolm has been very kind to me."

"He certainly has. You wouldn't be here now if it weren't for him."

Truer words had not been spoken. The sudden appearance of Charles Richards had caused a lot of trouble and raised more questions than answers. At first, he was accused of being George Betterman and Sheriff Hounslow had demanded that he be locked up. He was for a night, until Malcolm produced a plethora of medical and dental evidence from his vast archives to prove that Charles Richards was not Betterman, in spite of the fact that they looked the same. He'd even shown how George Betterman had once been mistaken for Charles Richards thirty years ago.

Predictably, Hounslow refused to accept any of it. Fortunately, the judge did and released him to Malcolm's custody. Malcolm, in turn, arranged to get Charles set up with a network of counselors working in Hancock, including Dr. Amos, to help him readjust to "being back." And soon, Elizabeth would be coming to see Dr. Amos as well.

Dr. Amos continued, "If what Malcolm suggests is true, your experience — along with Elizabeth's — could change everything we understand about time and space."

"No doubt," Charles replied.

"But I don't know how many people will believe him." Dr. Amos sighed. "You understand that we are just beginning the long and painstaking work to help you. You've been gone for over thirty years. And while I can't professionally accept Malcolm's explanation about time twins and time transference and everything else he theorizes in these pages — " he put this hand on one of the stacks of files " — I can work with you as someone who has suffered some sort of trauma that has caused what we might call your 'disassociation' from your past."

"In other words, you're saying I have amnesia."

"A form of it."

Charles smiled. He felt a strong sense of déjà vu, and knew not to argue.

"Our network will help reacquaint you with your life."

Charles looked at his cup of coffee again. The black liquid shook gently. "What about my wife?"

"We've found her — but she doesn't know about your return." Dr. Amos frowned. "We have to do this very carefully, Charles. For everyone's sakes."

Charles paused, his eyes still lowered. "Is she married?"

"No. She's widowed."

"And my children?"

"Grown. Married."

"Do I have grandchildren?"

"Charles, honestly — "

"Why not tell me?"

"Because you can't simply show up on their doorstep, not after all this time."

"You don't want me to have false expectations — hope."

Another sigh from the doctor. "Right."

"Whatever happens will happen in God's timing."

Dr. Amos stood up and stretched out his hand to shake his, indicating that their meeting was over. Then Dr. Amos placed his hands on the stacks of files. "Look, Charles, it would be better if you didn't talk openly about ... well, any of this time travel stuff."

"People will think I'm crazy."

"Exactly."

Crazy Charley. It had a nice ring.

Charles made his way out of the doctor's office, but hesitated at the door and glanced back at Dr. Amos, who was already looking at the file for his next case.

Funny, he was the spitting image of Dr. Forbes.

ripple effect

paul mccusker

Read chapter 1 of *Ripple Effect*, Book 1 in the Time Thriller Trilogy.

1

"I'm running away," Elizabeth announced defiantly. She chomped a french fry in half.

Jeff looked up at her. He'd been absentmindedly swirling his straw in his malted milkshake while she complained about her parents, which she had been doing for the past half hour. "You're what?"

"You weren't listening, were you?"

"I was too."

"Then what did I say?" Elizabeth tucked a loose strand of her long brown hair behind her ear so it wouldn't fall into the puddle of ketchup next to her fries.

"You were complaining about how your mom and dad drive you crazy because your dad embarrassed you last night while you and Melissa Morgan were doing your history homework. And your dad lectured you for twenty minutes about ... about ...." He was stumped.

"Christian symbolism in the King Arthur legends," Elizabeth said.

"Yeah, except that you and Melissa were supposed to be studying the ... um — "

"French Revolution."

"Right, and Melissa finally made up an excuse to go home, and you were embarrassed and mad at your dad — "

"*As usual*," she said and savaged another french fry.

Jeff gave a sigh of relief. Elizabeth's pop quizzes were a lot tougher than anything they gave him at school. But it was hard for him to listen when she griped about her parents. Not having any parents of his own, Jeff didn't connect when Elizabeth went on and on about hers.

"Then what did I say?" she asked.

He was mid-suck on his straw and nearly blew the contents back into the glass. "Huh?"

"What did I say after that?"

"You said ... uh ..." He coughed, then glanced around the Fawlt Line Diner, hoping for inspiration or a way to change the subject. His eye was dazzled by the endless chrome, beveled mirrors, worn red upholstery, and checkered floor tiles. And it boasted Alice Dempsey, the world's oldest living waitress, dressed in her paper cap and red-striped uniform with white apron.

She had seen Jeff look up and now hustled over to their booth. She arrived smelling like burnt hamburgers and chewed her gum loudly. "You kids want anything else?"

Rescued, Jeff thought. "No, thank you," he said.

She cracked an internal bubble on her gum and dropped the check on the edge of the table. "See you tomorrow," Alice said.

"No, you won't," Elizabeth said under her breath. "I won't be here."

As she walked off, Alice shot a curious look back at Elizabeth. She was old, but she wasn't deaf.

"Take it easy," Jeff said to Elizabeth.

"I'm going to run away," she said, heavy rebuke in her tone. "If you'd been listening — "

"Aw, c'mon, Bits — " Jeff began. He'd called her "Bits" for as long as either of them could remember, all the way back to first grade. "It's not that bad."

"You try living with my mom and dad, and tell me it's not that bad."

"I know your folks," Jeff said. "They're a little quirky, that's all."

"Quirky! They're just plain weird. They're clueless about life in the real world. Did you know that my dad went to church last Sunday with his shirt on inside out?"

"It happens."

"And wearing his *bedroom slippers*?"

Jeff smiled. *Yeah, that's Alan Forde, all right*, he thought.

"Don't you dare smile," Elizabeth threatened, pointing a french fry at him. "It's not funny. His slippers are grass stained. Do you know why?"

"Because he does his gardening in his bedroom slippers."

Elizabeth threw up her hands. "That's right! He doesn't care. He doesn't care how he looks, what people think of him, or *anything*! And my mom doesn't even have the decency to be embarrassed for him. She thinks he's adorable! They're weird."

"They're just ... *themselves*. They're — "

Elizabeth threw herself against the back of the red vinyl bench and groaned. "You don't understand."

"Sure I do!" Jeff said. "Your parents are no worse than Malcolm." Malcolm Dubbs was Jeff's father's cousin, on the English side of the family, and had been Jeff's guardian since his parents had died five years ago in a plane crash. As the last adult of the Dubbs family line, he came from England to take over the family fortune and estate. "He's quirky."

"But that's different. Malcolm is nice and sensitive and has that wonderful English accent," Elizabeth said, nearly swooning. Jeff's cousin was a heartthrob among some of the girls.

"Don't get yourself all worked up," Jeff said.

"*My* parents just go on and on about things I don't care about," she continued. "And if I hear the life-can't-be-taken-too-seriously-because-it's-just-a-small-part-of-a-bigger-picture lecture one more time, I'll go out of my mind."

Again Jeff restrained his smile. He knew that lecture well. Except his cousin Malcolm summarized the same idea in the phrase "the eternal perspective." All it meant was that there was a lot more to life than what we can see or experience with our senses. This world is a temporary stop on a journey to a truer, more *real* reality, he'd say — an *eternal* reality. "Look, your parents see things differently from most people. That's all," Jeff said, determined not to turn this gripe session into an Olympic event.

"They're from another planet," Elizabeth said. "Sometimes I think this whole town is. Haven't you figured it out yet?"

"I like Fawlt Line," Jeff said softly, afraid Elizabeth's complaints might offend some of the other regulars at the diner.

"Everybody's so ... so *oblivious*! Nobody even seems to notice how strange this place is."

Jeff shrugged. "It's just a town, Bits. Every town has its quirks."

"Is that your word of the day?" Elizabeth snapped. "These aren't just *quirks*, Jeffrey."

Jeff rolled his eyes. When she resorted to calling him Jeffrey, there was no reasoning with her. He rubbed the side of his face and absentmindedly pushed his fingers through his wavy black hair.

"What about Helen?" Elizabeth challenged him.

"Which Helen? You mean the volunteer at the information booth in the mall? That Helen?"

"I mean Helen the volunteer at the information booth in the mall *who thinks she's psychic*. That's who I mean." Elizabeth leaned over the Formica tabletop. Jeff moved her plate of fries and ketchup to one side. "She won't let you speak until she guesses what you're going to ask. And she's never right!"

Jeff shrugged.

"Our only life insurance agent has been dead for six years."

"Yeah, but — "

"And there's Walter Keenan. He's a professional proofreader

for park bench ads! He wanders around, making people move out of the way so he can do his job." Her voice was a shrill whisper.

"Ben Hearn only pays him to do that because he feels sorry for him. You know old Walter hasn't been the same since that shaving accident."

"But I heard he just got a job doing the same thing at a tattoo parlor!"

"I'm sure tattooists want to make sure their spelling is correct."

Elizabeth groaned and shook her head. "It's like Mayberry trapped in the Twilight Zone. I thought you'd understand. I thought you knew how nuts this town is." Elizabeth locked her gaze onto Jeff's.

He gazed back at her and, suddenly, the image of her large brown eyes, the faint freckles on her upturned nose, her full lips, made him want to kiss her. He wasn't sure why — they'd been friends for so long that she'd probably laugh at him if he ever actually did it — but the urge was still there.

"It's not such a bad place," he managed to say.

"I've had enough of this town," she said. "Of my parents. Of all the weirdness. I'm fifteen years old and I wanna be a normal kid with normal problems. Are you coming with me or not?"

Jeff cocked an eyebrow. "To where?"

"To wherever I run away to," she replied. "I'm serious about this, Jeff. I'm getting all my money together and going some-where normal. We can take your Volkswagen and — "

"Listen, Bits," Jeff interrupted, "I know how you feel. But we can't just run away. Where would we go? What would we do?"

"And who are you all of a sudden: Mr. Responsibility? You *never* know where you're going or what you're doing. You're our very own Huck Finn."

"That's ridiculous."

"Not according to Mr. Vidler."

"Mr. Vidler said that?" Jeff asked defensively, wondering why their English teacher would be talking about him to Elizabeth.

"He says it's because you don't have parents, and Malcolm doesn't care what you do."

Jeff grunted. He didn't like the idea of Mr. Vidler discussing him like that. And Malcolm certainly cared a great deal about what he did.

Elizabeth continued. "So why should you care where we go or what we do? Let's just get out of here."

"But, Bits, it's stupid and — "

"No! I'm not listening to you," Elizabeth shouted and hit the tabletop with the palms of her hands. Silence washed over the diner like a wave as everyone turned to look.

"Keep it down, will you?" Jeff whispered fiercely.

"Either you go with me, or stay here and rot in this town. It's up to you."

Jeff looked away. It was unusual for them to argue. And when they did, it was usually Jeff who gave in. Like now. "I don't know," he said quietly.

Elizabeth also softened her tone. "If you're going, then meet me at the Old Saw Mill by the edge of the river tonight at ten." She paused, then added, "I'm going whether you come with me or not."

Forbidden Doors

A Four-Volume Series from Bestselling Author Bill Myers!

Some doors are better left unopened.

Join teenager Rebecca "Becka" Williams, her brother Scott, and her friend Ryan Riordan as they head for mind-bending clashes between the forces of darkness and the kingdom of God.

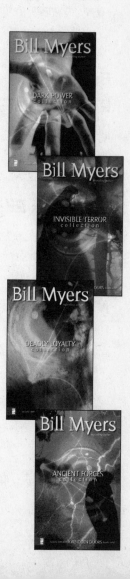

Dark Power Collection
Volume One

Softcover • ISBN: 978-0-310-71534-4

Contains books 1–3: *The Society, The Deceived,* and *The Spell*

Invisible Terror Collection
Volume Two

Softcover • ISBN: 978-0-310-71535-1

Contains books 4–6: *The Haunting, The Guardian,* and *The Encounter*

Deadly Loyalty Collection
Volume Three

Softcover • ISBN: 978-0-310-71536-8

Contains books 7–9: *The Curse, The Undead,* and *The Scream*

Ancient Forces Collection
Volume Four

Softcover • ISBN: 978-0-310-71537-5

Contains books 10–12: *The Ancients, The Wiccan,* and *The Cards*

The Rayne Tour

by Brandilyn Collins and Amberly Collins!

A suspenseful two-book series for young adults written by bestselling author, Brandilyn Collins, and her daughter, Amberly. The story is about the daughter of a rock star, life on the road, and her search for her real father.

Always Watching
Book One

Softcover • ISBN: 978-0-310-71539-9

This daughter of a rock star has it all—until murder crashes her world. During a concert, sixteen-year-old Shaley O'Connor stumbles upon the body of a friend backstage. Is Tom Hutchens' death connected to her? Frightening messages arrive. Paparazzi stalk Shaley. Her private night-mare is displayed for all to see. Where is God at a time like this? As the clock runs out, Shaley must find Tom's killer—before he strikes again.

Last Breath
Book Two

Softcover • ISBN: 978-0-310-71540-5

With his last breath a dying man whispered four stunning words into Shaley O'Connor's ear. Should she believe them? After two murders on the Rayne concert tour, Shaley is reeling. But she has no time to rest. If the dying man's claim is right, the danger is far from over.

Coming October 2009!

Visit www.zondervan.com/teen